ALLISON ROSE

The Nameless

Tales of an Outcast Faerie Part One

To my mom,
and to Ashley,
the first to believe

Contents

Prologue	iii
Chapter 1	1
Chapter 2	6
Chapter 3	13
Chapter 4	21
Chapter 5	24
Chapter 6	30
Chapter 7	37
Chapter 8	44
Chapter 9	49
Chapter 10	55
Chapter 11	58
Chapter 12	67
Chapter 13	71
Chapter 14	75
Chapter 15	84
Chapter 16	88
Chapter 17	92
Chapter 18	99
Chapter 19	103
Chapter 20	107
Chapter 21	116
Chapter 22	120

Chapter 23   127

Chapter 24   132

Chapter 25   136

Chapter 26   139

Chapter 27   145

Chapter 28   149

Chapter 29   155

Chapter 30   160

Chapter 31   162

Chapter 32   164

Chapter 33   168

Chapter 34   171

Chapter 35   178

Chapter 36   180

Chapter 37   186

From the Author   192

Acknowledgments   193

About the Author   194

Also by Allison Rose   195

Prologue

All life begins and ends with the *ara*, the life force within all living things.

It connects man, beast, and faerie to the natural world.

It is a magic that must be nurtured and protected.

This was true for the land of Earth once, when man and faerie lived in peace beside each other.

Over time, the humans began to pull away from the natural world and their faerie brethren.

They grew so far from magic that they forgot its existence and denied it altogether.

No longer able to live in such a place, the first faeries withdrew from Earth, creating a world of their own.

The world known as Faerie now remains connected to Earth by a single magical pathway. Only the rulers of Faerie hold the key.

The human world became merely a story to those of Faerie; the few who were forced to cross to the human world were those who committed the unforgivable.

The outcasts.

Chapter 1

Forevermore an outcast.

The words echoed in Kelty's mind as laughter drew her gaze to a human family among the visitors of the park below. Resentment and longing burned in her chest at their smiling faces, yet she could not look away. Landing with light feet on a branch high above the field, she folded her wings to her back as a long sigh escaped her lips.

The sun shone upon on the woods of the human world, casting a brightness upon the leaves. But despite the brilliant green, the fresh air, it paled in comparison to the world of Faerie.

Kelty took a breath as the homesickness hit her. Sinking into a crouch, she reached inward to the magic at her core and sent some of it through her bare feet into the rough bark. Connecting to the *ara*, the life energy within the tree, she used the steady, soothing presence to ground herself.

The *ara* of this world was weak, but it was starting to respond to her. Nurturing and caring for the energy of the land was all she knew how to do in this place of banishment. What little life existed in the plants, trees, and soil now glowed brighter, healthier to her vision. She was doomed to be its only champion.

Kelty's eyes followed the two human children, a boy and a

girl, as they squealed and chased each other around in the lush grass. Their movements were a little awkward given their small stature, but their fun continued regardless. Two adults watched the children attentively from a picnic blanket, looking on with indulgent smiles.

To see such joy at the simple connection with the world around them, proof that not all humans were entirely apathetic and destructive, should have inspired relief in Kelty. This day, the sight only served as a reminder of the life she lost, the future now out of reach.

The comfort she drew from the *ara* of the tree drained from her, the memories she worked to keep down surfacing despite her efforts to forget.

Forevermore an outcast.

The family blurred as tears clouded her vision. The judgment decreed by none other than her father, Baron of the Night, haunted her to this day, as did the pain of knowing she did nothing to deserve her banishment. Bitterness filled her as she recalled her mother's face, stoic but for the pain in her eyes. Her father's expression was nearly blank, as if distancing himself from the words he spoke. They knew of her innocence, yet they could do nothing to stop her from being cast out of her home. Her actions were unforgivable.

Kelty blinked away the last image she had of Faerie, forcefully wiping a hand across her eyes. She exhaled in an attempt to ease the painful knot in her chest.

No. I will not dwell on it. There was nothing to be done now except wait and maintain her distance from humankind, the warning from the stories her parents told her always at the forefront of her mind.

Contact with humans drains faerie magic.

Strengthening the *ara* of the wood and keeping watch on the humans from far above kept Kelty's magic strong and hope alive within her heart. Her mother would clear her name in Faerie and come for her. And when she did, Kelty would be waiting.

It would happen. It had to.

A shrill laugh brought her out of her thoughts. Kelty focused back in on the family just as the young boy caught up to the girl, giving her a tap on the arm. The girl squealed in what seemed to be delight at the game, though she lost her balance and toppled over onto her backside.

No... Kelty flinched, a hiss coming to her lips as the action triggered a different memory. Phantom fingers clutched at her arm as a face of blue swam before her eyes, devious smirk a sign that he knew he had her trapped. This hadn't been an innocent game. Their contact broke the rule, the one that must never be broken.

Partnership between those of the Night and those of the Day was banned after one such couple sought to combine their opposing magic, causing a backlash of power that killed all the members of both courts and nearly destroyed all of Faerie. The Silver Dusk.

The blue one carefully crafted the trap that resulted in Kelty's banishment. He was of the Day and she of the Night. Though it was the first time she ever laid eyes on this faerie, the touch of his magic within her left no question of their involvement, a perfectly crafted illusion that they intended to enter into a partnership that echoed that of the Great Destroyers, the ones responsible for the Silver Dusk.

Kelty had no time to react to the violation, her family happening upon them as he grabbed her arm, speaking the words that

3

would awaken his magic within her. There was nothing she could say that would prove her innocence as she was examined by those with the affinity of spirit that could sense the magical bonds between potential partners.

His magic was cleansed from her, their potential bond dissolved, but nothing could erase the damage to her name. The unforgivable cannot go without strict punishment, especially for the heir of the Night.

Forevermore an outcast.

Kelty's heart pounded and she pressed her lips into a hard line as the memory taunted her. She did not know what became of the blue one. The Day took him away to pass their own judgment on him. But if she ever saw him again, he would suffer for taking everything from her.

The leaves around her rustled in an unsettled whisper, as if a breeze were present despite the stillness of the air.

Kelty took a breath and unclenched her fists, withdrawing her magic back into her core so that the trees would no longer feel her anger. She stood then, wings twitching with an overwhelming need to fly, to get away from the painful reminder of what she was: a fallen star.

She spread her wings as she turned from the family, but just before her feet left the branch, Kelty paused as an uncomfortable sensation caused her to shiver, like that of eyes watching her.

The human girl sitting on a bench at the edge of the field looked down hurriedly as Kelty's eyes zeroed in on her, bending her auburn-colored head over a book that was open in her lap. She wore simple garments in typical human fashion of pants in shades of blue and a white top. By her smallness and delicate features, Kelty guessed she was young. Unremarkable.

A quick glance of the area revealed that no other human eyes were looking up at her. Some of the tension left Kelty's body as she exhaled. The magic that concealed her from human sight was present in a soft caress against her skin.

Turning away from them all, Kelty vaulted into the air as if she could escape her fate.

Chapter 2

Nola's eyes followed the faerie's actions closely, her pencil now still in her hand.

Trying to draw her always turned out to be a vain effort, but something drove Nola to try, time after time, to capture the true beauty of the purple, silver-haired being whose wings shimmered in the sunlight.

The wings in particular were difficult to capture from so far away. They were shaped like those of a butterfly with two slightly overlapping sections on each side, membranous material outlined by what looked like veins of a slightly darker silver-gray. When the faerie wasn't on the move, she typically had them collapsed flat on her back. And when she flew, the wings became a silver blur. The color of the wings was hard to get as well. Nola didn't have a colored pencil called moonlight.

It was as if the page could not contain her. A human-made flimsy piece of notebook paper could never hope to contain the faerie's otherworldliness.

Her clothes were at least easy to get right. She wore a simple, light brown fabric wrapped around her body; the tight cloth covered her from her shoulders to her knees, yet allowed her to move her legs without being revealing. Her long silver hair spilled over her shoulders and her feet were bare. A true being of nature. Nola came to think of her as the forest spirit, the guardian of the wood.

And, hopefully, the one who could help her out of a mess of dark magic and threats.

As far as Nola could tell, she was the only human with the ability to see the faerie. No one else in the park showed any signs of seeing anything out of the ordinary during the few weeks Nola spent observing, testing out her new sight.

It was the worst night of Nola's sixteen years of life, the night a strange gray substance was forced down her throat by a group of eighteen-year-olds from school. The end result was a power of sight that Nola had to admit was pretty cool despite the horrible way it came about.

She now saw glowing lines of energy in the natural world, flowing through the ground and up through the trees and plants. The faerie herself was a being of light to Nola's vision. She spread the light outward as she healed the plants and trees around her, their leaves, flowers, and branches growing stronger and brighter. It brought a sense of peace to the park and to Nola. The discovery of the faerie was the best part of her abilities.

Yet, I still don't have the courage to speak to her.

In truth, the beauty of the faerie intimidated Nola, as did her apparent disdain for humans. She avoided the visitors of the park, flitting in and out of the branches above their heads in movements so graceful the leaves barely moved. The few times the faerie gave even the slightest attention to the humans below was to sneer at them. Or at least that's what Nola thought she witnessed from afar.

Nola made trips to the park after school and on weekends, watching and waiting for some sign that the time was right, that there might actually be a chance the faerie would understand her. And this was beginning to feel like the right time.

The pencil bit into her hand as her grip tightened. Nola's position on the bench afforded her a view of the faerie that was close enough to see her facial expressions while remaining enough to the side to make her look inconspicuous.

Today, the faerie was staring down at a family of four. Two children played tag as their parents watched over them. There was a look of rapture on the faerie's face as she stared down at them. The next moment, her eyes filled with tears and she wiped at her eyes with one arm. Yet she continued to look down upon the family, features hardening, silver brows creasing into something like anger or jealousy.

Nola actually checked again to make sure the family wasn't doing anything out of the ordinary. *Nope. Just a normal game of tag. This is the most emotional reaction yet.* Excitement coursed through Nola. *A human reaction.*

Those beautiful wings flicked restlessly a couple times, catching the sunlight as the faerie stood. Nola hurriedly looked down as sharp silver eyes turned toward the bench she sat on. The faerie wavered for a second, the leaves around her rustling. Heart pounding, Nola kept her head down until the flash of purple from the corner of her eye indicated the faerie had flown away.

It has to be now.

Nola dumped her notebook in her pack and rose from the bench. Squinting up into the sunlight, she focused in on the energy of the trees, which flowed in lines up from the ground and through the branches. The faerie ran her hands along the bark of the trees and leaves as she passed, leaving a touch of energy visible to Nola, as if the tree held in just a bit of her energy for a moment before fading away. Sometimes the leaves almost seemed to bend out of her way, allowing the faerie, who was slightly smaller than the average human, to move through the trees with incredible grace.

Nola followed the trail of faint purple bursts. She attempted to look normal as she avoided others walking on the path.

I will just start by saying hello. I will do it this time.

Her knuckles tightened on her pack as she hurried along. The gravel crunched under her sneakers, tripping her up a few times as she concentrated on the trees above. She refused to think about the possibility the faerie had never interacted with humans before.

She obviously cares for the wood. If she understands English, she will at least hear what I have to say.

Adjusting her pack, Nola picked up her pace a little.

I wonder if the faerie knows she leaves a trail when she moves, Nola thought, trying to distract herself from the twisting in her stomach. *Or that anyone else is able to see it. Maybe she doesn't care. Maybe it is as natural as breathing to her.*

The shade replaced the afternoon sunlight, and the air grew cooler as the trail led Nola to the back section of the park that was designated for the preservation of nature. *Like that wooden gate is a barrier to anyone who really wants to get in.* The faerie frequented this area to the point Nola wondered if she lived back there.

The presence of a tour group walking towards Nola forced her to pause at the barrier. She paced, pretending to wonder at the nature all around and the sky above as they passed. *Come on.* Agitated, she kept the glow in one corner of her eye. When they finally disappeared around the bend, she vaulted over the barrier and ducked into the bushes, coming out on the other side just in time to catch the faerie's trail again.

I'm quite comfortable with breaking the rules these days. Not that the workers of the park ever really come back here. Nola rolled her eyes as she continued forward.

Lost in thought as she was, the sight of a familiar dark figure nearly gave her a heart attack as she rounded a bend in the trail. *What on earth?* Nola quickly ducked back behind a tree, holding her breath. Peering back around, she just caught the tail end of a black cloak before it disappeared into the wood.

Nola let out her breath, but her heart continued to pound. Only a few idiots would walk around in a black cloak in broad daylight on a warm day. *Not now*, she thought squeezing her eyes shut. *What could Derek possibly be doing? There is no meeting today.*

She glanced reluctantly back to the fading magical trail and heaved a frustrated sigh. *He is too dangerous. If I walk away and he destroys the woods right now, it will be my fault.*

I guess meeting the faerie will have to wait. Again. But I will try to contact her right after I figure out what this psycho is doing.

Dread was a knot in her stomach as she carefully crept from tree to bush behind the tall, cloaked figure, desperately trying to keep far enough back and remain quiet. Playing in this wood as a child, Nola had practice placing her feet so as to avoid twigs and leaves, but she was painfully aware of the swish of her jeans as she walked. She was forced to duck behind larger tree trunks several times when Derek stopped suddenly to survey the wood. Some leaves and brambles started to take up residence in Nola's hair and catch on her clothes. She tried to brush them off while still being alert.

What is he doing? Nola's throat tightened as she came upon the obvious answer. *He has to be testing something. And if he's doing it alone, it must be bad.*

Derek was the leader of the group that forced Nola to swallow the substance that caused her enhanced vision. He used his position as an intern working for Nola's father, a biochemical scientist, to steal the substance from the basement lab. Derek also used it to make other, far more dangerous substances, the worst of which instantly destroyed anything living, disintegrating it into nothing.

Nola remembered the day Derek's group showed the black substance to her. They chose a lily from the pond near where they usually met. Ice-cold fear had run through her veins as the flower disappeared in an instant, leaving an empty space in the world.

And I am a part of it now. Shame colored her cheeks. She hadn't been a part of the dark magic's creation, but she now went to the meetings of the group she called the cloaks, forced by threats of violence upon her friends if she refused. Derek suspected the substance, the gray power as he called it, affected Nola despite her denial. She was his greatest experiment.

And hopefully his downfall, Nola thought, reminding herself that her position within the group may just give her the knowledge she needed to take them down before they destroyed every living thing around them or sold the dark magic to someone else who would.

Nola ducked behind some bushes as Derek halted abruptly in a clearing that was, oddly, in a patch of sun. Peering carefully around the thick branches, Nola's heart rose into her throat as Derek pulled out a knife from the folds of his cloak. He stepped forward and slashed a horizontal line into the bark of a large tree. Then he moved on. She flinched each time he made contact, fighting a gut feeling that told her to retreat. He

11

made quick work of it, his cloak swinging open as he gouged each tree in a wide circle.

A glint of sunlight on glass that came from within the folds of Derek's cloak caught Nola's eye.

No, no, no. He has some of the vials.

Backing into the center of the clearing once more, Derek brought out a matchbox as well as a vial containing a familiar, swirling black substance. The breath left Nola's lungs as if it was sucked out of her.

He's going to destroy the wood.

Chapter 3

Kelty fanned out her wings and landed in a crouch on a tree branch, head cocked to one side. A sharp current resonated up through her feet, and the magic at her core stirred in response.

"Humans have such a fascination with destruction," she seethed as she took off, allowing the trees to guide her to the source of the disturbance. Taking mental stock of the power within, she made sure the magic that would camouflage her purple skin and silver wings with the leafy background was in place. The last thing she needed was a human spotting her because of carelessness.

An eeriness came over her as she chose a perch high among the leaves and zeroed in on her target. A lone cloaked figure stood below. The cruel marks in the circle of trees around him was the source of the disturbance.

Tucking her wings close to her back, Kelty dropped silently to the ground, coming around behind one of the tree trunks in the circle. The cloaked human remained with his back to her, fiddling with something in his hands.

The sting as Kelty touched one finger to the gouge in the bark sent the magic within coiling into her center once more. She snatched her hand back, finger still burning as a tinge of darkness threatened to seep into the rest of her. Hurriedly,

Kelty backed around the tree and buried her finger into the soil. Connecting to the *ara* beneath, she drew more magic into herself and drove out the tinge of black in her hand, the soil of the human world absorbing it.

Her extremities grew cold, though the danger had passed. There was only one explanation.

This one has iron.

It was a weapon she only heard spoken of in hushed tones when stories of the humans were told back home. Iron, the metal that smelled much like the tang of human blood, was a poison that would seep into a faerie, destroying from the inside the magic that kept them alive.

Suppressing a hiss, Kelty's eyes flashed daggers at the cloaked human as she removed her hand from the soil.

Two courses of action lay before her: apprehend the human and risk her life, or watch as he destroyed the land around them.

Before her banishment, the choice would have been easy. The purpose of faeriekind wove endlessly through her thoughts. *Care for the land as it cares for us in return.*

But this wasn't Faerie. She had no obligation to this world. And this human had a weapon that could kill her with one touch.

The figure removed his hood to reveal a boy of youth with a thin face and sunken eyes. Kelty quickly jumped and wove through the branches to get a better look as he removed an item from his cloak. The boy flicked a small wooden stick against a box until it came alive with flame. Eyes lighting up in his otherwise expressionless face, he waited until the fire almost touched his fingers before flicking his wrist to put it out.

Kelty froze. The few months she spent in the human world were enough to realize how reckless humans were with fire.

A coldness, like the chill of death, washed over her as the

boy opened a small vial in his other hand. A black substance was just visible through his fingers. It swirled with a mind of its own, content within its container for now, but roiling with disastrous potential. Kelty leaned back, eyes wide and a hand over her mouth.

It was like no magic that existed in Faerie. And as far as she knew, humans had not been able to sense or use magic for a long time. There was none left within them. At least that is what they taught in Faerie.

Death...a magic that feels like death. Kelty slipped from the tree to the ground. *How—how does it survive?* All magic in Faerie was connected to the *ara* and all living things. It could not be bound to the air.

Suddenly the boy flicked one of the sticks into a flame once more and waved it over the vial of dark magic. The result was a visible dark cloud that swept outward away from the human. An intense burning energy rocked through her, shooting up from the ground at her feet. Kelty shut her eyes and dropped low as the *ara* within her recoiled, sinking into her core. Then an awful quiet fell over the wood.

Kelty forced her eyes open despite the dread in her heart. The trees within a few paces in front of the human were charred and black, lifeless husks. The *ara* within the soil continued to disappear before the faerie's sight, a darkness spreading to other trees, infecting them from the inside. She watched them wither, leaves dropping and bark growing brittle and flaky. Smoke clouded the air.

The devastation ceased once it reached a shallow pond a short distance away, leaving behind an emptiness, a pocket of death.

Tears ran down Kelty's cheeks. She began to shake in fear and fury.

Death is all these humans bring to the world of life.

She leapt up into the air, breaking contact with the darkness beneath her feet. Perched again among the leaves, she reached out with her magic, anchoring herself into the branch she rested on. Grounded in life, the tree's energy a soothing balm, she turned determined eyes on the boy of dark magic.

Life belongs to every living thing. It is not yours to destroy.

With his back still turned to her, the boy examined the charred remains before him with eager fingers, the vial once more tucked out of sight.

Kelty inhaled a steadying breath and then slid to the ground again. She couldn't think of any magical attack that would be effective against the strange darkness. This wasn't faerie magic.

Her only choice was to take it from him until she could figure out what to do with it.

The boy couldn't see her through the magic she kept wrapped around her, and she could get close enough to grab it from his cloak. The plan was risky, especially since he had the knife of iron, but a magic that dangerous did not belong in the hands of humans.

Care for the land as it cares for us in return.

Kelty stepped forward, withdrawing the magic inward that she wasn't using to conceal herself from human sight. It would not be needed for what she was about to do.

The chill of death on her skin intensified as she came within a few paces of him. His cloak hung partially open, as he still had his arm extended to examine the remains of the tree before him. Her gaze locked onto the vial containing the awful magic.

"Derek."

The voice startled the boy into turning sharply. Kelty ducked backwards to avoid being struck by the boy's movement, retreating back farther to be safe. *Moon above*, she cursed silently.

Kelty glared at the newcomer, a girl of youth with a round face and large eyes, possibly about the same age as the boy, though she was much shorter. Her blue pants and white T-shirt were a brightness next to the darkness of the boy's wardrobe.

There was something familiar about the girl's small stature and auburn hair. Kelty shifted to her right and peered closer.

The girl with the book. The one she thought was staring at her.

Wide hazel eyes caught Kelty's attention. And then those eyes looked straight into hers.

The breath froze in Kelty's chest at the first being to truly look at her since her arrival months earlier. There was a mild surprise, but also a recognition amongst the warm kindness and fierce determination in their hazel depths. Vulnerability, confusion, and fear all coursed through Kelty, making it impossible to move or think, a moment frozen in time.

Then she broke free from the shock. *Impossible!* Kelty jerked back into the brush. The flow of her magic was ever present in a caress of her skin. The girl should not have been able to see her. And she was not nearly startled enough by the sight of a being so unlike humankind.

Kelty's heart began to pound. *How...* Her thoughts spun, but there was no denying it. The girl had seen her through her magic. Closing her eyes a moment, she tried to relax. *No, this cannot be happening.*

A short bark of laughter drew Kelty's attention back to the boy. Tearing herself out of her thoughts, she focused back in on the humans.

Dangerous, both of them.

17

Kelty took to the trees once more, carefully avoiding those affected by the dark magic, to gain a vantage point directly above the two.

The expression on the boy's face—Derek, the girl had called him—was that of a predator toying with prey as he approached the girl, but she stood her ground.

"What are you doing here, brat?" he asked, his tone somehow both annoyed and mildly excited.

"I could ask you the same thing." The girl put her forearm over her mouth as she coughed, wide eyes roaming over the devastation behind the boy. "What—what did you do?"

"You can sense it?" Derek stalked forward.

"I can't breathe, that's all." The girl frowned and stepped back, eyes still wide with horror.

Kelty couldn't help but be intrigued by the girl. *She is not excited by the dark magic like this violent one.* She peered closer at the strange human. A soft pulse of light lived in the girl's chest, what the faerie called the core.

There is a touch of magic to this one.

Derek continued his advance as he reached into his pocket and withdrew the knife.

Kelty jerked back at the flash of sunlight on the blade, cursing inwardly as her finger burned with the memory of the iron poison.

"Derek, don't." The girl stepped back with one foot, but didn't flee.

In one quick movement, he had the knife pinned to her throat.

"What did you sense just now?" he demanded in a low voice.

The girl called "brat" glared up at him despite the fear apparent on her face.

"I smelled smoke," she said. "Are you *trying* to set the woods on fire?"

The knife trembled in Derek's grip. "Tell me the truth," he demanded, ignoring the last comment.

"That is the truth."

There was a beat of silence. "I don't think it is," Derek said quietly. Then he lashed out with a quick flick of his wrist, leaving a small cut on the side of the girl's neck. Eyes wide, the girl rushed to cover it with her hand.

Such violence towards the innocent. Kelty turned shocked eyes on the human boy.

"Perhaps you will think about it and tell me your real answer later," Derek said rather casually as he examined the trickle of blood on his knife.

The human girl merely stared with wide eyes, one hand still pressed to her throat.

"Think long and hard." Derek gave her a look that seemed like pity. Then he tucked the knife into his cloak and strode off into the woods.

After releasing a gasp that sounded more like a sob, the girl ran off in the opposite direction.

Moon above. Kelty dropped to the ground, swinging her head between where the girl went and the opposite direction of Derek's path.

Dark magic first. Her sharp eyes found the cloaked boy as he retreated through the wood.

Placing a hand on the tree behind her, Kelty felt through the network of energy for the strand connected to a large branch directly over Derek's head. With a hiss, she magically willed it to snap in two, causing the heavy branch to collapse. It hit its target, startling an angry cry out of Derek as it pinned him to the ground.

With a small relief that the vial did not break upon impact, Kelty urged the magic still remaining in the branch to grow and bend. *Please, one final task*, she pleaded as she coaxed the smaller offshoots to wind their way around the vial of death magic and stealthily remove it from Derek's cloak before he threw off the branch.

Derek threw a glare at the tree as he righted himself. Then he slunk away, pulling his hood back over his head to hide his spooked expression. Kelty bared her teeth silently at his retreating back.

Tears stinging in her eyes, Kelty flew over to retrieve the vial of death. *Many thanks, sturdy one.* She placed a hand on the tree's trunk, magic flowing from her to heal the damage she had caused up above. It was the first time she asked for such a sacrifice, and it was an honor that the tree responded so readily. *Necessary, necessary,* she chanted in her mind. It didn't help to assuage the guilt.

Kelty closed her fingers gingerly over the vial, fighting the gut response to throw it or to get away from it somehow. The inky black continued to swirl slowly despite her feelings towards it.

How would the humans have gotten such a magic? Why would they even think of using it? What kind of magic does the girl have?

Kelty snapped back to the situation at hand. Spotting a group of rocks several paces away, she piled them to form a cage around the vial, binding the rocks together with a magical seal.

The death magic would have to wait. She must find the girl who could see through her faerie magic as no other human had.

Chapter 4

He actually pulled a knife on me. And he used it! The shocked thoughts ran through Nola's mind as she ran. *That psycho could've killed me.*

Gut burning, Nola slowed to a stop and ducked behind some foliage. Panting, one hand over her neck and the other over her mouth in an attempt to quiet her breathing, Nola listened for the sounds of Derek's pursuit. The tension left her body as only birdsong and the rustle of leaves met her ears. *Maybe he made his point for the day.*

Removing her pack, Nola slid to the ground in an ungraceful heap. She leaned back on the trunk of a tree and closed her eyes. The sounds of the birds chirping overhead began to soothe her, but her heart refused to slow.

As silent tears fell down her cheeks, she removed her hand from her neck. A thin trickle of blood covered her palm. *Not that serious.* Despite her relief, her shaking hands made it difficult to find her gym shirt in her pack to tie it around her neck.

I stood up to Derek. I stood up to him when he was alone. I thought it might actually stop him, that I would save the day or something.

Her beating heart refused to still as her thoughts ran in circles. Now Derek suspected even more that she was hiding a secret, that she really was changed by the substance he forced her to swallow. Up until now, he seemed content watching and threatening. Now, he might do more to discover what she was hiding, what power it was he gave her.

Nola pressed the shirt to her wound as she turned her thoughts to forming a plan. *The forest spirit, she knows about him now. And she knows about me.* A little excitement seeped into her state of shock. *She saw me. At least there is that, even if it did seem to spook her.*

Despite her injury, Nola was glad the faerie got to witness that encounter. *I hope I looked like the good guy. Maybe she will be more willing to speak to me now.*

Nola heaved a sigh, then winced as her wound stung from the movement. She still needed to talk to the faerie, to truly explain the danger. She might have already waited too long.

A twig snapped not far off. Nola jumped to her feet and spun toward the noise, eyes darting around her. The sight of a figure far off into the trees nearly sent her running, but then she noticed the bright red of the man's sweatshirt. She breathed out as she put one hand to her chest, continuing to survey her surroundings.

Derek might still be here somewhere. I can't be alone with him again. Flight instinct almost took over again at the thought.

Then reason kicked in for one precious moment. Nola pulled her notebook out of her pack.

I really hope the forest spirit can read. She quickly scrawled a note to the faerie, shoving it in the hollow knot of a nearby tree along with her pen.

Nola placed her hand over the hole, fingers brushing the roughness of the bark. *Please let her see this.*

A sudden rustle in the leaves spurred her feet back onto the path and toward home.

I'm talking to trees now. I'm one step closer to crazy. But if it will help... She readjusted the shirt over her neck, trying to hide some of it with her medium-length auburn hair.

No living thing is safe with Derek and that magic around. I have to convince the faerie to help.

Chapter 5

The trees guided Kelty down the path the girl ran, their energy recognizing the magic-touched human's. The trees lit up one by one, showing Kelty the way.

The girl called "brat" sat alone beneath a cluster of trees, writing clumsily in a notebook, a beige garment wrapped around her neck. A few spots of bright red dotted the fabric.

Kelty landed among the leaves, high enough to watch while remaining hidden. Down below, the bushes moved ever so slightly to surround the girl, their energy reaching out to her.

She peered at the girl's center once more. *What sort of creature is she?* As before, the small glow marked this one as different than other humans, but unlike any magical being Kelty knew of.

Something pulled her towards this girl, but Kelty shook her head sharply at the dangerous notion.

Humans are a poison, even if they seem magical.

The problem remained that this one saw Kelty through her concealment magic. She needed to find out what kind of danger this girl might put her in.

Initiating contact was a danger in itself, though. The more time spent with humans, the more a faerie's magic would disappear. It was unclear exactly how it happened, but to remain faerie, Kelty must avoid humans at all costs.

Humans were not welcome in Faerie. Neither were outcast faeries turned human.

The biggest problem before Kelty was whether to initiate contact for the purpose of discovering the girl's intentions or remain unseen in the safety of the leaves and hope for the best.

Impossible, the life of an outcast.

Kelty slid down the tree in an attempt to get close enough to read the words the girl was writing, but before she got close enough, the girl ripped out a page and shut the notebook.

Straightening, while clumsily shouldering her pack, the girl glanced around and above in furtive movements. One hand pressed to the garment around her neck, she inserted the rolled-up paper and her writing implement into a hollow knot in the tree Kelty occupied. Then the girl closed her eyes for one moment, her round face relaxing and becoming more child-like as she rested her fingers on the bark. A slight warmth flared beneath Kelty's feet.

Her eyes widened. *Humans do not speak to the trees.*

Kelty wrestled with indecision for a moment as the girl hurried away. She seemed harmless. *How could anyone who speaks to the trees be dangerous?*

But her time as the heir of the Night taught her to never let her guard down. *Some things are not as harmless as they seem.*

Kelty flew after the girl, keeping under the concealment of the leaves. *More care is needed with this one. But for now, whatever she is, I can watch from afar. There is not enough cause to speak. Not yet.*

The girl cut through the brush on the wilder side of the wood, tripping a few times as she ducked under and around overgrown foliage, casting more furtive glances behind her. Kelty paused a few times, ducking out of sight despite the fact the girl was looking behind and not up.

She is more afraid of the boy than an unfamiliar creature. Kelty recalled the recognition in the girl's gaze as they locked eyes. *How long has she been watching? What has she seen?*

The questions burned in her mind, but the risk of revealing herself to this human was still too great.

Their journey ended at a dwelling near the outer parts of the wood. With one last look over her shoulder, the girl shut herself safely inside.

Tread carefully, girl called "brat."

Kelty turned back, making the return trip to the tree that held the message as the sky turned to dusk. In the fading light, she paced the ground, her head level with the hollow knot that contained the note.

She clenched her hands against the temptation to take it. Though it appeared to be the safer route than speaking with the girl, the risk was still great. Reading that paper meant flirting with the line between purity and poison, a dangerous game.

Faerie tales taught her that interaction with humans was forbidden in order to keep the magic alive, the *ara*, the life force within them and all around. That was it. There was no guidance for what she should do if she ever came into contact with a human that could see her, had a touch of magic within her, and left her a note.

Kelty's feet stilled and she faced the rough patterns of bark on the ancient tree. She lifted one arm, her fingers hovering over the knot, inches from the crumpled paper.

An ache started in her chest as she thought of home and the fact that if she took this step, she might be sucked so far into the human world that there would be no hope of escape. But

Derek's pale face replaced the visions. Her wings twitched at the memory of the chill of that dark magic as the boy unleashed it upon the wood.

The note may contain information about that dark magic, information that might mean the protection of the wood she nurtured with such care, the *ara* that kept her alive.

Letting her breath out through her teeth in a hiss, Kelty plunged her hand forward to retrieve the paper. With shaking hands, she smoothed it open.

Her eyebrows rose in pleasant surprise that the humans still used the same language as her kind. Squinting at the messy scrawl, she read the words:

To the nameless forest spirit,

Please help me stop him. I can't do it on my own. And there are others. They created that substance. And they can make more. They must be stopped before they destroy the woods. And possibly you. Maybe even mankind.

Please help.

Nola

Kelty flexed her wings, hands clenching the paper. *Please help,* echoed in her mind.

Unfair to ask this of me, human girl. She thrust the note back into the hollow knot and vaulted into the air.

She didn't stop, climbing up through the leaves until she was just under the treetops, so far from *them* that she could think clearly. Settling in the crook of a branch and tucking her wings to her back, she closed her eyes.

No, this cannot be happening. The one shred of hope Kelty had of returning to her past life felt like it was slipping from her

27

fingers, her kind heart pulling her toward the human conflict though her mind pulled away.

Human matters are no concern of mine, she thought with vehemence. Their race was a lesson about what happens if one loses sight of magic.

But defeat crept into Kelty's mind as she thought of home, and the hope she might return. It seemed to grow farther from her as the days went by. *They have not come for me yet. What if they never come and I am forced to become a part of this world?*

The thought startled her into opening her eyes. Guilt immediately burned inside her, and she wrapped her arms across her stomach. The faces of her mother and father flashed across her mind. Her sister. All faerie of the Night that looked up to her. She was the heir of the Night, the Star.

In Faerie, she was someone. She had a purpose. She belonged. And surely she would belong again once her family proved her innocence, and once she proved her strength by surviving the human world with her magic still intact.

No, I cannot give up on my home.

With one hand, she parted the leaves above her to reveal the face of the moon, her guide. It paled in comparison to the Great Light, the moon of Faerie, but its soft glow washed over her and soothed any remaining indecision from her mind.

Faerie is where I belong.

Her mother's words came to her as she gazed upward. *Wait and watch and do what you can until the time is right. Never, never strike unless you can win.*

Bracing herself on the trunk to her back, Kelty rose to her feet.

One human's plea is not enough of a reason to sacrifice my being. I will wait until they come.

28

With a tired sigh and a hardened resolve, Kelty tucked her wings close and dropped on light feet from branch to branch on her way to the ground.

It was about halfway down that the *ara* within the tree grew brighter, more intense, as if from contact with one more powerful than itself. She came to a halt, pressing herself against the bark, eyes wide.

Faerie.

The emotions coursing through her were equal parts hope and fear. Either her kind had come for her or someone had come for a much darker purpose. Kelty gave her head a quick shake. *I will have to face them either way.* Gathering her magic, she slid the rest of the way down the tree to face what waited below.

Feet landing lightly in the soil, she sent her magic down through the ground, searching, probing.

Only the traces of another faerie lingered, fading slowly from the *ara.* One spot, though, one burst of energy drew her eyes to the bark in front of her.

Kelty tensed as she beheld the mark coaxed into the tree bark, the same tree in which the human girl placed the note. A crescent moon, the symbol of the Night. The energy emanated a gentle warmth, calling to that within her. With shaking fingers, she reached forward to press her hands to the rough moon shape. The essence of the other faerie enveloped her, bringing with it the fresh scent of soil. A current of magic made its way up her arm, and she heard the words in her mind. A smooth, male voice.

Faerie that refuse to protect the life around them do not deserve to be called faerie.

Chapter 6

Nola resisted the urge to finger the bandage as she snuck back into the woods the next night, the glow of the energy around her lighting her way through the dark. She trudged down the path to the old hunting cabin the cloaks, as she called them, used as a meeting place. The gravel crunching under her feet sounded too loud. The dread in the pit of her stomach increased with every step.

She wanted nothing more than to run to the tree where she left the note, but hadn't dared go back in case she lured Derek there. He had a disturbing ability to pop up without warning.

I believe in life and goodness, and the best way to save it all is to watch them and discover what they are up to, she reminded herself with a deep breath.

All she could do was continue to play dumb and hope it worked again.

A flashlight illuminated the ground in front of a tall hooded figure leaning against the wall of the cabin.

"Have you considered telling the truth?" Derek asked when she tried to walk past him. "Admit the gray power affected you somehow. I can sense something different about you. You might as well just admit it."

Nola swallowed and spoke past the lump still in her throat.

"I told you the truth. If you don't want me around, just say the word." She meant for the words to come off flippant, but her voice wobbled. Clamping her mouth shut, she hurried toward the door.

"You would miss the fun." His sarcastic words drifted to her as he followed.

She turned and ducked into the small space, a lantern throwing shadows on the walls and sparse wooden furniture. The place wasn't much of a comfort. The stuffiness made Nola want to rush back out to the fresh air and the life outside.

Derek strode in and brushed past her toward the table at the back of the room, dropping his interrogation for now. It was both a relief and a message that he thought he was so powerful that her words didn't matter. It was possible he didn't even need an answer. At least not yet. He knew his threats would keep her around until he got what he wanted.

"Your friends might make good test subjects," he had said to her that first night in the cabin after he forced the gray substance down her throat; she had lied to his face, saying she felt fine. Derek suspected the opposite and used the threat to keep her quiet and around for his study.

Nola hadn't spoken to either Tris or Lauren in weeks, ever since that night. It was better that way. They were safe.

He probably thinks in time I will slip up anyway. Nola fiddled with her cloak as she kept Derek in the corner of her eye. *He is enjoying this game.*

Adam, Derek's right-hand man, and Jeanine, the tall beauty who graced Derek's arm, hardly glanced her way. Cameron, though, did a double take at the sight of the bandage, concern causing lines in his perfectly smooth skin. Nola's heart gave a little stutter. *He noticed.*

"What happened to your neck?" Cameron bent his perfect blond head forward, as if that might help him see through the bandage.

Nola opened her mouth and froze, her gaze darting involuntarily to Derek.

"The brat is extremely clumsy," Derek said snidely without turning his attention from the table.

"I...fell," Nola said, her voice sounding lame even to her own ears.

Both Jeanine and Adam snickered from their places on either side of their leader. *Mindless lackeys.* Cameron nodded slightly, blue eyes still suspicious.

Derek turned abruptly then. The two by his side immediately straightened and flipped their hoods back over their heads. Cameron gave Nola a small, sad smile as he did the same. Though she knew it was an empty gesture, Nola's shoulders relaxed ever so slightly as she joined the circle.

Derek stood with his back to the fireplace and lit one match with a furious strike, as he did to begin all of their meetings. Silence settled like a blanket over the room for a few long seconds as they watched the flame burn through the tiny wooden stick.

With a flick of his wrist, Derek put out the flame. In another quick motion, he flipped his hood back to reveal his long face, sunken eyes, and crooked nose.

They all removed their hoods and Derek spoke.

"The black power and fire combined is not what I hoped. Leaves a mess behind."

Nola's breath caught at the matter-of-fact way he described the devastation he brought upon that area of the wood.

Across from her, Adam flinched. "You tested without us?"

32

he asked.

Derek gave him a dismissive wave of his hand. "There was no time."

Adam's dark eyebrows nearly rose up into his messy hair. "Have they moved up the timeline?"

Nola zeroed in on Derek for his reaction to the odd phrase. *Who's they?* She shifted her feet at the thought there may be someone else involved.

But their leader merely gave his second a hard look before launching into the next order of business.

"Next...we try the red power on a human," he said, a glint in his eyes.

Nola's stomach lurched. "A live one?" she blurted out.

Jeanine gave her a look of disdain. "Obviously, a dead one."

Nola was too stunned to glare at the older girl whose sneer seemed to be a permanent feature on her face. There had been talks of getting a cadaver, but she didn't think they would go through with it. *And what are they cooking up that they want to try out on a human body anyway?*

The group tested other substances out on various plants and small mice they trapped. Nola only watched. It was all a game of trial and error, mixing human chemicals in with the gray substance. The cloaks took great care in keeping the exact ingredients from Nola, but made sure she witnessed the effects of their experimentation. Most of the mixtures hardly produced any effect, but that brought Nola little comfort.

This is the first I am even hearing of this red one. She shifted her feet. *I hope it is not as horrible as the black death.*

Nola opened her mouth to ask about it, but Derek cut her off. "No more questions."

No, no, no. I can't stop this if I hardly know what is happening.

She straightened and opened her mouth again.

Then the knife was out again and pointed at her face. The dim light of the lantern glinted off the sharp edge.

"Derek," Cameron said, almost whining, while shifting from foot to foot. Jeanine looked down at her fingernails in boredom, while Adam watched with his head tilted in fascination.

"Behave," Derek warned as he put the knife down.

Nola tensed at the order, but kept her mouth shut. Anger at him and at her own helplessness swirled in her gut. *The less attention he pays to you the better,* she reminded herself. *He will get what is coming to him. Eventually.*

"Actually, you are dismissed for now." Derek picked the knife back up, a hardness in his eyes. He waved it towards the door. "Leave. Go on."

Are you kidding me? Nola bristled at being talked down to like a child. All three of the others looked surprised at the sudden turn of events.

No, no, no. I need to know what they are planning.

"And if I want to stay?" she shot back at him, nearly choking on the words.

Without a word, Derek took a menacing step forward. Fear shot through her as she hastily stepped backward. "Fine." She backed off, hating herself for her cowardice, but not knowing what else to do.

Nola kept all of them in sight as she fumbled with the door. Cameron at least looked apologetic. *Not that it helps any.*

She shut the door with a slam, an action that felt childish in the next moment. With a harsh sigh, she automatically took off toward home, thoughts a mess of anger and confusion.

I should just tell my father and bow out now. Maybe Derek will even go to jail or something. Then she shook her head with a sigh. *Who am I kidding? Derek's father's corporation has enough money to be above the law. They'll find some way to pin this on Dad. They'll fire him and it would be my fault. And then the wood will suffer and the forest spirit—*

Wait. This is my chance. Nola turned and took off in a run toward the opposite direction from home.

Please, please, please, she thought as she reached the tree where she had left the message. Her breath came in short pants as she removed the paper with careful fingers.

Unshouldering her pack, Nola sat and propped her phone up on the ground for light. Her hopes soared as she flattened the note. But after scanning the words she wrote, she found nothing else.

Tears of frustration pricked at Nola's eyes. *I don't know why I put so much faith into this faerie. I don't even know exactly what she is.*

That gut feeling remained, though, the confidence that the faerie could help. Nola just had to convince her.

It's probably my fault. I wrote that note quickly. It was vague and probably sounded too desperate. Or maybe she can't even read English. But I have to try again.

She reached into her pack for a pen. Turning the note over, she paused and considered what to write this time.

A flash of green out of the corner of her eye startled her out of her thoughts. Heart in her throat, she jumped up and spun toward it. The normal noises of the woods at night, the clicking of the bugs and the occasional rustle of leaves as the animals of the night moved about was all that met her ears. Her eyes only picked up the strands of energy she witnessed on a daily basis.

She relaxed a little, but still remained on edge. *I'm so jumpy these days. It was probably an animal.*

The animals of the wood glowed, too, though theirs was different than the plant life, more centered around a ball of energy that radiated outward rather than focused at the base.

Nola sat again, retrieving her phone and propping it up once more. It took another few minutes of pondering before she finally decided, *Well, I can invite her to see the madness for herself.*

This time, she simply wrote:

The cabin shortly after the sun sets.

Capping her pen and retrieving her phone and her bag, Nola put the note back into the knot. Carefully making her way down the path to the farther side of the lake, she bent down and gently removed one of the smaller pink lilies that dotted the water. The flickering light in the window of the cabin across the lake caught her eyes as she stood. Nola gave it a glare.

This will lead the forest spirit to the cabin, and what she sees there will convince her if the note will not.

Chapter 7

In the quiet of her home tree, Kelty stared at the swirling black that was visible through the clear glass of the vial in the palm of her hand.

The stillness of the air and the soft glow of the Telk stones that were placed into the wall created the illusion of night. Within this tree that she had grown and nurtured to a size large enough that she could lie flat on the dirt floor, she could almost imagine that she was back in Faerie.

Though being in this space relaxed her body and soul, just looking at the black substance caused the energy within her to recoil inward, life seeking to be as far away from death as possible.

Faerie that refuse to protect the life around them do not deserve to be called faerie.

The words were a taunting she couldn't ignore. *I am not refusing entirely,* she thought, pushing the voice aside. *I am facing this dark magic.*

In Faerie, magic was bound to living things and stored in stones called Telk that allowed the faerie to use magic that wasn't part of their affinity. Though those with the affinity with air could temporarily infuse the air with magic, the effect would not remain. Water may be the element of binding, but there wasn't enough moisture in the air to bind a magic this intense.

I may have to go further. A different sort of fear grew within her then. It was a familiar fear, one that made her want to curl up into a ball and deny her own existence.

She held the rare power over all of the affinities: land, water, sun, spirit, air, and beast. The only one born this way in hundreds of years. The Star of the Night.

Only those closest to her knew of this secret. And for her survival, it must remain that way. If the Day found out, she would become the target of attack and torture. Her power threatened the control they had over Faerie. It might one day restore the balance, but for the entirety of her nineteen years of life, Kelty's parents made sure that she only used her other affinities with them in private, secure locations.

Now, mindful that many of risks of this world were unknown to her, Kelty was still careful to only use her power with the land, the power that she was known to possess. That familiar fear of exposure drove her to resist the temptation of using her secret power.

But as she stared down this magic that spread death like nothing she had ever seen, she pushed past the fear. *I have to do this.*

Kelty focused on the dark swirls, gathering her magic and forcing it to the forefront of her mind. *The Star does not break before any magic, especially human magic.*

Taking a deep breath, Kelty opened herself up to the air around her, withdrawing from the *ara* of the land that kept her anchored. This was her least favorite of the affinities, the floating sensation unnerving. Kelty's lips curled into a snarl as she probed the substance tentatively with a strand of her power. The black gave off an essence that was faerie-like and also distinctly other, almost having a human, iron-like feel to it, like the metallic-smelling blood that ran through human veins.

Kelty gasped as the power she probed with instantly drained upon contact with the dark magic. There was no pain, but the sensation of life being sucked out of her, like there was no air left to breathe, was disturbing beyond imagining. Kelty abruptly let go of the air and grounded herself in the land, withdrawing her magic tightly within.

Wrong. The substance felt distinctly wrong, unnatural. And she couldn't figure it out.

With shaking hands, she wrapped the vial once more in a tight casing of woven reeds and stones that she infused with a magical seal. It would keep the death from seeping out and affecting the *ara* of the wood, the life beyond her home tree. Giving herself a little push off the floor with her wings, she stored the vial on a ledge higher up inside the tree. The farther away from the ground, the better.

Then she pushed open her wooden door, rushing out into the sunlight, for once its brightness more of a comfort than the cool darkness of her home tree.

Kelty closed her eyes and tipped her head back as she shook out her wings, trying to rid her body of the chill. She focused on the life energy around her, the sounds of the animals rustling the leaves on the ground, the distant voices of humans.

The air suddenly grew moist, bringing with it the scent of spring rain and a sense of magic that danced over her skin. Kelty's eyes flew open. *What in the name of the moon—*

Whirling around, she placed her hand on her home tree, the magic that would conceal it flowing from her.

A soft chuckle reached her ears as he dropped out of the trees to land lightly across the clearing. Another chill spread through her at the sound.

No. He cannot be here.

A smirk crossed Briar's delicate features as he folded his wings and straightened. The darkness of his wings and his long, flowing black hair made his blue skin seem lighter and his beautiful eyes a shade of darker blue. The symbol of the sun, a black swirl with jagged lines radiating from it, visible from beneath the strands of his hair marked him as one of the Day. A dark cloth was wrapped tight around his lithe and graceful body so that only his arms and feet were bare, creating a vision that would tempt any faerie.

Forcing her spine straight, Kelty locked eyes with the one who caused her banishment. She held her magic at the ready, but Briar made no move to attack, taking on a casual stance with crossed arms. The chill within her turned into a slow burn as her fingers clenched.

"Beautiful day," Briar said in his soft, sultry voice as his eyebrows arched mockingly.

Her magic stirred within at the memory of his taunting voice in her ear, daring her to risk her life to help a young faerie of the Day, to overstep her bounds, and to walk straight into the trap he set for her. She remembered the coolness of his magic as it crawled inside her and for a brief moment touched the magic at her core as only potential partners could do. It was a violation and also evidence of the unforgivable, the intent for one of the Day and one of the Night to accept their potential relationship and become partners. Briar's motivations for the act were unclear. Kelty had never laid eyes on him before then and had no contact with him afterward, only learning his name through others as they examined her before her banishment. The whole thing was perplexing and infuriating.

In brief moments of rage and self-pity, Kelty had wished she would meet Briar in this world to get the answers she could not puzzle out on her own.

But now that he stood before her, all she could think about was that he dared show his face after taking everything from her. There wasn't even a hint of fear or remorse behind his smirk.

The rules are different now. Kelty closed her hands into tighter fists against their trembling. *He must think he still has some power over me.*

In trepidation, she focused her gaze on his core. A touch of relief coursed through her veins as no sensation took over, no light or warmth. Their connection as potentials was truly broken.

But then what is he doing here?

Kelty ignored his casual greeting, folding her arms and giving him a fierce glare. "You have been banished as well?" she forced out.

Briar inclined his head. "We committed the unforgivable."

"*You* committed the unforgivable," Kelty nearly shouted at him. "I did nothing."

Dark blue eyes regarded her calmly. "Think that if you wish."

Kelty took a breath and swallowed the urge to scream as she gave voice to the question that haunted her still. "Why did you do it?"

"I think you know the answer to that."

There were many theories that ran through Kelty's mind on a daily basis, the most likely of which was that the Day wanted her out of Faerie. *I got too close, overstepped my bounds. I was a threat.* Her thoughts were merely speculations, though, useless without proof.

"Why did you do it?" she repeated in a tight voice.

Briar gave her a small sigh. "It was your own doing."

She stalked forward a step, eyes flashing. "I saved lives."

He titled his head, eyes still taunting her. "The Day don't see it that way."

Kelty breathed out slowly in an effort to release the tension inside her. *I need to know if he knows of my abilities, if the Day put him up to it. If he has knowledge that could destroy me.* Her lips parted to demand answers, but he spoke first.

"Stay away from the humans," he warned, the taunting edge to his voice gone.

Every muscle in Kelty's body froze. "What do you know of the humans?" she asked past the fear threatening to choke her.

The smirk came back and his eyes glinted. "I cannot tell you that."

He knows at least something of my involvement. Kelty's jaw clenched and her heart pounded. *Knowledge can always be used as a weapon.* "What is so important about these humans?" she tried again.

"You've seen enough. Any more will taint you beyond return." Briar gave her a knowing look.

He spoke sense, but the implication that she should listen to him, that he knew what was best for her, sent a shiver of fury through her.

This time Kelty did strike out at him, being careful to use only her power over the earth and growing things. The branch closest to the infuriating faerie instantly grew to twice its size and lashed out toward the delicate wings on his back, a warning.

But the branches clutched only air as Briar disappeared, his body disintegrating completely.

So he is one of those. The slippery ones. The ones that were powerful enough to dissolve themselves into the moisture in the air around them.

Kelty let out a cry of frustration. *Why? Why is this happening?*

Withdrawing her magic into herself, she retracted the branch, coaxing it back into a normal position.

Just a few days ago, she was the lone faerie of the wood. Now two strange faeries were asserting their unwelcome opinions.

A watcher who dared to suggest it would be wrong to refuse the girl.

And an enemy, who dared to warn her away.

Neither of them had the right to tell her what to do. And both knew too much about her for comfort.

She paced the small space in front of her home. *If only I could talk to Mother or Kallyn. Just talk to them.* Tears pricked at her eyes at memories of her mother and sister and their sometimes challenging but honest guidance.

I don't know what to do.

Chapter 8

Nola startled awake the next morning, panting and unclear why her sleeping self had been so agitated. Wincing, she realized the bandage on her neck had become tangled in her hair overnight.

At least it isn't bleeding anymore. Looking in the bathroom mirror, she arranged her hair to cover it. The circles under her eyes were a normal thing now. Her normally round face had slimmed down with worry; her eyes took on a look of lost innocence. *I look older now,* she marveled at her reflection. *I'm not sure if that's a good thing or not.*

Anxiety started to bubble up from her stomach. Nola walked back into her room in search for the one thing that steadied her these days, other than walking in the wood. She reached into her pack, thrown carelessly onto the floor last night, for her notebook.

Panic spread as her searching hands came up empty. *I had it last night. I know I did.* She always had it. The feeling of being able to put pen to paper and sketch these things that no one else saw, things that no one else would believe existed if she told them, comforted her like nothing else would.

Nola turned to search the room. *No, no, no. What if someone found it? What if Derek found it?* She pushed those thoughts aside as she searched. It was too awful to contemplate.

After searching the room twice, there was still no sign of it. Frustrated tears formed in her eyes.

"Nola!"

She startled at the sound of her mother calling her. Nola swallowed.

"Yes?" she called in a voice that sounded stronger than she felt.

"Are you coming down?"

Nola ran a hand over her face as she remembered. *Right. Saturday brunch.* It was something her mother started, fearing the family wasn't spending enough time together. *Which is true. She just doesn't know the half of it.*

"Morning," she said moodily as she rounded the bottom of the stairs and into the kitchen.

"We have a guest today," her mother said cheerily in response.

Nola stopped short. "A guest? Who?"

Her mother turned from the stove. She wore a brightly-colored button-down shirt and slacks, and her blond-brown hair was pulled back. She gave Nola a once-over as only a mother could. "You might want to change."

Looking down at her oversized T-shirt and pajama bottoms, Nola sighed and trudged back upstairs. *I'm not putting on anything more than jeans. Whoever this person is can deal with it.*

After putting on clean jeans and a fresh T-shirt, she made her way down the stairs once again. As she crossed the kitchen to the sliding glass door that lead to the back deck, she heard his voice through the open window.

Nola froze. *Are you kidding me? This can't be happening.* The urge to turn around and go right back upstairs nearly overwhelmed her.

45

Her mother turned her head then, catching sight of Nola through the glass. With a smile, she waved her forward.

No, no, no. But Nola pasted on a smile and forced her feet forward. *The only way out of this is to act normal. You are good at that now.*

Her father, who she silently referred to as the Scientist, and her mother sat at opposite sides of the table, and between them sat Derek. *Like one happy family,* she thought incredulously. *How on earth did he get invited to Saturday brunch?* The older boy was not a stranger to the house, given he was her father's intern and sometimes spent time in the basement lab, but being invited to a meal meant for family time was something Nola never thought her parents would extend to him.

Nola sat stiffly across from Derek. He looked almost normal without the cloak, sporting a black T-shirt and black jeans. But there was no amount of normal clothes that would cover up the creep factor in his gaze. He merely gave her a nod, stoic expression in place.

"Derek tells me you kids have a new benefactor for your project," the Scientist beamed at her in complete ignorance. The sun painfully revealed the pasty tone of his skin as he squinted.

So that's it. Derek has come to throw something in my face. Something I didn't know. Probably the they *who Adam let slip last night. And my dad invited him with open arms.* She really couldn't fault the Scientist for that. It was how Derek played it off. And Nola had to agree the less her father knew, the better.

Nola forced another smile onto her face. "Yes," was all she could muster. Derek's eyes glinted at her from across the table. Nola managed a slight glare at him. "They are quite interested in our work, aren't they?" she added slowly, keeping her eyes on Derek.

Noticing, and misinterpreting, the Scientist gave her a sideways smile that made her want to vomit. "You two should be so proud."

Derek remained silent, refusing to give anything more away.

Nola's mother smiled at her. "Derek says you'll get to show off your project soon. Nola, you didn't tell us you were that close to something."

Nola choked on the bite of scrambled egg she had just forced into her mouth. As she coughed, she looked up to see Derek's satisfied expression.

So something big is happening soon.

"I didn't actually think we were there yet," she said, keeping an eye on Derek's face.

"No need to be modest," was Derek's cool response.

And he won't even give me a time. Why did he even come here?

But she knew. It was a way to demonstrate his power over her. *Sadistic jerk,* Nola fumed as she tried to control her facial expression.

"That's great," she said, tightly. Her mother gave her a suspicious look, but the Scientist keep on eating, looking rather pleased with himself.

Dad has no idea what is going on around him, she thought in exasperation. *If only I could tell him that it was his magic gray substance that caused all of this. And that there is no way I'll ever be friends with Derek.*

Once, all she ever wanted from her father was for him to be pleased with her. Now that he was, she didn't want it. It felt wrong.

But she couldn't disappoint him even more with the truth. It wouldn't do anyone any good.

The rest of brunch passed with only light talk between them. Nola hardly said a word, mind churning over this new turn of events. Derek hardly said a word either, apparently having accomplished what he came for.

When Derek went to leave, he paused at the door. "I will see you tonight, Nola," Derek said in a suggestive voice that made Nola want to turn and run in the other direction. And when the door clicked shut after him, she did.

Nola just caught the secretive glance her parents exchanged as she rushed past them and back up the stairs. *Let them think I'm embarrassed,* she thought as she shut the door to her room. *They only ever see what they want to see. They don't see the real me. No one does. I'm trying to use that to my advantage, but it's so hard.*

Chapter 9

The birds sang as Kelty set out the next morning. She gave them a glare as she wove through the trees, as if the small creatures had any right to be cheery.

She had tossed and turned under her woven blanket most of the night, thoughts of the human girl and the two male faeries tormenting her.

When Kelty opened her eyes after catching what felt like a few minutes of sleep, it was with purpose.

There was one side of the story she knew nothing about, and one who could provide her with answers.

Today, she would find the watcher.

Dropping lightly to the ground, Kelty folded her wings and stepped forward to run her fingers over the crescent moon shape the watcher coaxed into the message tree. The energy was faded to almost nothing, the *ara* of the human world absorbing the life in it. But as before, she detected calm and strength, distinctly male, and the shadow of a scent that reminded her of fresh soil.

She detected no animosity from the energy despite the stern message it bore. Yet, he was watching her in a wood of the human world without showing himself.

Strange, this faerie.

Now reminded of his essence, she took to the trees once more. She sought out the largest, oldest trees. Running her hands along the bark, she sent her magic down through their network of roots in search of traces of the watcher—the one who knew about the human girl and indirectly urged Kelty to risk her magic, her very being, to help.

The sun made its way across the sky and the air grew hotter as she searched.

And when she made it full circle to the message tree, there was no trace of the watcher faerie.

He is good at covering his tracks.

With a defeated sigh, Kelty collapsed onto the ground, back to the rough bark, wings carefully splayed out on either side of her.

One thing was certain: His gift with the land was as powerful as hers, making it easy for him to disguise himself when he didn't want to be seen.

Either the watcher faerie lived beyond the wood as an outcast, or he still lived in Faerie. It was enough that Briar, now an outcast, knew of the human that begged her for help. A resident of Faerie could ruin her name further, her chances of claiming innocence in the face of Briar's cruel trick, of returning to the life she loved and missed with an ache that threatened to consume her.

The tree at her back emitted a comforting flow of energy in her direction. It was a minimal amount, but Kelty's frustration eased slightly.

She rose to her feet with a sigh, and just as she was about to take off, a flash of pink caught her attention. She turned back to the message tree.

A single lily sat within the hollow knot.

The girl had been there.

With gentle hands, Kelty reached into the crevice and pulled out the flower. She traced the delicate, long petals, moist despite being on land. It was one of those that grew in a pond on the far side of the wood.

The *ara* was still alive in the flower, which meant it had been plucked from the water recently. What the girl meant by this was unclear.

Kelty peered back into the hollow knot to see that the note was still there. Brows furrowed, she tucked the lily into her hair, infusing the roots into the silver strands so that the flower may live, and unfolded the worn paper.

The cabin shortly after the sun sets.

Kelty read the words over again. Then it came to her.

The place of dead wood along the lily waters. Kelty glanced at the sky. The sun sat just above the horizon.

It was not too late.

Faerie that refuse to protect the life around them do not deserve to be called faerie.

Kelty closed her eyes and let out a long, weary sigh, her decision made. It may have been made long ago.

This time will be different, she vowed as she glided through the trees to the pond. *At least it is the opposite of what the blue one wants.*

* * *

All seemed quiet as Kelty landed on a high branch to look down over the calm waters. The place of dead wood was visible across the way. The cabin, Nola had called it. The pond had a serene feel to it, the landscape often drawing the visitors of the park. The soft light of the setting sun only added to the beauty of the pink flowers that dotted the surface.

Kelty traced the petals in her hair as she sent her power down through the tree, searching for anything unusual.

The plant life around the pond grew fertile and lush, the water filled with fish and other animals. But as her awareness reached the other side of the lake where the cabin loomed, she found the oddity she was looking for. No roots grew underneath the structure, as if the trees shied away from it.

She flew closer to the cabin, keeping cautiously to the trees. The only humans in sight were across the pond, a couple walking hand-in-hand closer to the path than the cabin. Dusk meant they would soon be leaving as the park closed.

So what happens here after dusk? Kelty wondered.

On careful feet, she crept forward to peek into the windows of the cabin. It was dark and empty. For now.

Removing the lily from her hair with gentle fingers, Kelty walked the few paces to the shore and knelt, placing it back into the water.

Live on. She gave it a little burst of energy.

The faint smell of fresh soil and a quiet, familiar energy flared behind her as she released the flower.

Every bit of her tensed, and in one fluid motion, Kelty tucked her wings close to her back and spun around, magic gathered at her core and ready to strike. The pulse of energy drew her eyes to a spot amongst the leaves above.

For one long second, her eyes met a pair of brown ones. His green skin nearly matched the leaves around him, the darkness of the color a sign of strength. The symbol of the black crescent moon that marked him as one of the Night was visible on his right temple. She caught a glimpse of brown wings behind him and his long brown hair hung in a braid over his shoulder. A strong jaw and smooth skin, along with rich brown eyes that seemed to stare right through her, gave him a look that made it impossible for Kelty to think clearly, other than two words of recognition.

The watcher.

Silently, with that stoic expression still on his face, he reached up to grab a stone that hung around his neck. A light surrounded his hands and spread until he was consumed by it. In the next moment, he was gone.

"Wait," the word came out of Kelty's mouth softly, too late to be heard.

The breath rushed out of her in a frustrated cry. She vaulted high up the nearest tree, resting shaky hands against the rough bark as she settled among the leaves.

He returned to Faerie. He belongs there. He will not even speak to me. He knows about the humans.

Kelty squeezed her eyes shut and tried to quiet her mind. After a few long minutes, she took a deep breath and opened her eyes again.

The fact that he had a Telk stone that could travel between worlds meant one of the rulers of Faerie had given it to him. Either her parents, the rulers of the Night, were looking for her, or the Day wanted to see her suffer.

This faerie was of the Night. Kelty had to believe one of her own kind would not betray her like that.

The frustration remained that she knew nothing besides this. And he departed again without saying anything.

Leaning her head back against the sturdy tree, Kelty inwardly cursed the males of her kind as she waited for the sun to set and for whatever the human girl wanted to show her to appear.

Chapter 10

I can't believe I really lost it, Nola fumed as she hurried to the cabin after spending as much time as she could looking for her notebook along the paths she would have taken last night. *Of all the dumb things—I just hope Derek doesn't have it.*

Trying not to cry like a child over a lost toy, she checked in and around the bushes and trees, near benches she frequented, and everywhere she had been in the last few days. Nothing. When the sun began to set, she reluctantly retrieved her cloak from her pack and slipped it on over her clothes.

Nola had cut off the bottom of her cloak in a stroke of rebellion so that it flared out like a skirt and, much to her relief, didn't get in the way of her legs as she hurried. It made her feel good to cut the fabric at the time. *Stupid, useless act,* she thought now. *It didn't help anything. Just like I'm not helping anything now.*

The cabin came into view as she rounded the bend, the skyline dim except for the fading light of dusk beyond the lily pond. Her heartbeat sped up like it usually did at the sight of the structure in the dim light, but she forced herself to move forward.

Just as Nola's sneaker hit the raised stone of the path to the door, a flash of brilliant blue out of the corner of her eye startled her to a stop. She whipped her head over to the left, just catching a glimpse of a blue winged being among the leaves a short

55

distance above.

This one appeared to be male with blue skin and long black hair that looked to be at least half tied up behind his head with the rest hanging over his shoulders. The tips of black wings were visible near his sides. A dark garment wrapped around him from his neck to ankles, but left his arms free, giving him a gothic sort of look.

He gazed back at Nola for one drawn-out moment with a self-satisfied expression before turning and ducking out of sight.

There are more of them. Nola's body remained frozen to the spot, extremities starting to tingle. *Where do they come from? Have they always been here? Have I just not bothered to look these past few weeks?*

Then a fear hit her. *What if they're not friendly?* The purple faerie gave off a peaceful vibe despite her distaste for humans. This one seemed a little more mysterious. The look he gave her was almost as if she were a toy he would love to play with. *What if these faeries are involved with so much more than I thought?*

Her heart pounded though the blue faerie was gone. Despite her fear, Nola's feet involuntarily moved toward the spot she had seen him.

The door to the cabin swung open, breaking the spell, and Cameron's perfect blond head poked out. "Nola?" he asked in a hesitant voice.

Nola's heart skipped a beat as she met Cameron's questioning gaze, heat rising into her cheeks. *He probably thinks I'm crazy.*

"Coming," she said quickly, hoping Derek hadn't witnessed that as well. *That's the last thing I need. Gosh, this is so messed up.*

Cameron waved her forward, a little hastily. Reluctantly, she pulled her hood up over her head and followed him inside.

The others gave Nola dirty looks from various casual positions around the room. *They waited,* Nola thought in surprise. Then the red drew her gaze to a vial in Derek's hand.

What do they want me to see?

Chapter 11

A noise broke the silence around the lily pond, the heavy steps of human feet on gravel. Kelty climbed up a few more branches for a better vantage point.

A hooded, dark figure approached the cabin. He glanced both ways before ducking into the entrance, giving Kelty a quick glimpse of his face.

She tensed as she recognized Derek. The paleness of his skin and sunken eyes were accentuated by the dim light.

Creepy, the humans call it. Kelty had learned many new words in the short time she had spent around mankind.

Frustrated and restless as she was, Kelty narrowed her eyes at him.

It is time for action. This I can do something about.

Determination creasing her brow, Kelty flew over to a high window. Pausing to ensure the flow of magic that hid her from human eyes was present, she then swung open the window and crawled inside, spreading her wings to glide softly down to the dirt floor.

Her eyes roamed over shapes of a human-made chair and table set and some other shelves and trunks. The wood that made the furniture was dead and dull to her senses, but a sort of throbbing energy drew her to a large stone structure on one wall. It had a gaping hole in the bottom center.

Derek busied himself with some papers that he pulled out of a box in one corner. After a glance at him, Kelty silently flew over to inspect the throbbing stone, keeping to the air.

The ash in the bottom marked it as a place where humans burned wood, but it also gave off an energy that made her skin tingle as it disturbed the magic within her. It reminded her of the black substance that leached the life out of the trees.

The more predominant energy, though, was coming from behind the stone at the back of the fireplace. When she touched the stone, an intense heat warmed the palm of her hand. It felt different than the black magic. This was too much energy in one place.

Magic like this was never meant for the likes of humans. Twisted. Twisted and unnatural, this magic.

The cabin door swung inward. Startled, Kelty banged her head on the stone, falling to land in the ashes. She just barely managed to suppress a cry of surprise.

Skin crawling, Kelty scrambled out of the remains of dead trees and ducked into the nearest corner. She dusted herself off in frantic movements.

Silently, three more black-robed figures filed in. *There are more of them,* she thought in awe and disgust.

They exchanged casual greetings and took up positions around the room. A boy with dark hair placed himself at the side of Derek, who was examining something on the table intently, while another boy with blond hair remained on the other side of the room, shifting from foot to foot. A tall girl examined her nails as she leaned against the table.

There was an air of impatience about the room, as if they waited for something. Derek straightened and strode over to the fireplace, black cloak swishing. When he ducked back out of the stone opening, he held another vial, this one a swirling red.

Wrong. Kelty squinted, eyes burning. *Too bright, this energy.*

The faerie grimaced as an unsettling feeling started in her gut. In a matter of seconds, breathing became almost impossible, and her magic recoiled further inward. Her vision swam before her eyes.

Kelty barely managed to crawl forward, concealing herself behind a wooden chest before all went black.

* * *

Hushed, bickering voices reached Kelty through a disoriented haze.

"Not that much! We only have one!"

"Yeah, dude, you'll fry it!"

"Guys. Shut up."

And then silence.

With effort, Kelty cracked open her eyes. *Twisted. Twisted magic.* Anger and revulsion colored her thoughts as her memories came back to her. Never had she felt so powerless. It was an effort to even think about moving, her limbs refusing to cooperate, her breathing labored. The *ara* within her was tightly coiled at her center, dull and retreated inward. *What in the name of the night...*

She winced as something nagged at her, something important she was missing. *Something is happening,* Kelty thought sluggishly. Summoning her strength, she managed to twist over onto her side toward the voices. Her new position afforded her a glimpse at the humans huddled on the other side of the chest.

Fear spread throughout her body as she eyed the dark-cloaked humans. The magic she had left was all that was sustaining her, that which concealed her from sight gone. If they even stood and looked over the chest, they would find her. And she wouldn't be able to escape in this weakened state.

No, please not like this. She watched helplessly as the humans leaned over something that was out of her sight. They murmured in hushed tones, though there was a note of excitement in the air. Peering closer, she realized they had removed their hoods. The blond figure closest to her shifted slightly and she caught sight of Derek.

Kelty renewed her efforts to move her limbs, her wings, trying to touch her magic. Her limbs remained barely responsive, the magic still coiled within, protecting itself and saving her strength. *Death at the hands of the humans.* An edge of hysteria wound its way through her thoughts.

Then she heard Derek's voice, alive with excitement. "The dead lives again!"

Kelty's eyes froze wide as she saw that he held a severed human finger. The relief that it was obviously not from any of the humans present was short-lived as the finger started to vibrate visibly. The color had been off, grayish and devoid of life, but started to gain a more healthy pinkish color. The noxious energy assaulted the faerie's senses, and she turned her head from the spectacle in a vain attempt to escape it.

The resulting explosion of power rocked through Kelty. Squeezing her eyes shut, she willed her magic even further into herself. A violent shiver wracked her body all the way to the tips of her wings. And then it was over as quickly as it had occurred, leaving her trembling.

Kelty remained curled up in shock for another moment, not even able to form a coherent thought.

"No!" a male voice yelled. "It was working! It almost worked!"

"Almost?" a female voice said in disgust. "Derek, it exploded. And it's all over my shoes!"

"Shh! Someone will hear us!" another female spoke sharply and quietly.

I know that voice. Coming out of her shock, Kelty slowly turned to her side as the humans continued to argue.

"No one is out here, brat," Derek snickered.

Brat...no. With dread, Kelty's eyes searched for the familiar voice.

"Whatever," the blond boy said in a calming voice. "Most of them don't work anyway. We will just try again tomorrow."

"Maybe it was too much," the boy with dark hair pondered.

"You didn't tell the benefactors it was ready, did you?" the whiny female asked.

At that moment, the feet belonging to the fidgety blond boy moved just enough to reveal a short girl with auburn hair, round face, and all-seeing hazel eyes.

Nola.

Kelty's fear kicked up a notch at the sight of the one who could see her, the one who wanted her to forsake her future to help her, the one who participated in this horror. Betrayal and disappointment at the one human who fought for the life of the wood, and her part in this mess, confirmed the choice Kelty made to stay out. The decision settled into her mind as the figurative distance between herself and the humans grew.

Violence and death is all they know. Dangerous, this girl who sees.

Attention returning to the scene before her, she just caught a glimpse of the whiny female as she breezed out the door. Derek turned on Nola, who stood twisting her hands in front of her, a look of shock on her face. "You can clean this up," he said in an accusing voice.

Cloak swirling as he turned, Derek flipped his hood up and strode out the open door. The other two followed suit, though the blond boy paused in front of Nola. His back to Kelty, she could only guess at the look he gave the girl. He said nothing. Nola's lips parted as if she wanted to say something, but then she pressed them together again. She turned away and went to the opposite corner. The blond boy turned towards the door, and with a shake of his head, he left, shutting the door gently behind him.

These two could not even find words for the horror that just occurred. Kelty tested her limbs once more, painfully aware of Nola's movements on the other side of the cabin. *Danger,* the word repeated over and over in her mind. She flexed her hands and feet. A small relief, but far from what she needed to escape. Frustration overwhelmed her. Beneath her, her wings twitched.

Life cannot be given back to the dead. Magic does not work that way. Stupid, meddling—

"You fell in the fireplace, didn't you?"

Kelty jerked and looked up, eyes blazing, to meet Nola's. She pressed her lips together, paralyzed by the alien sensation of the direct gaze of a human. Her heart pounded, magic stirring inside her, responding to the fear and the urge to run. She remained silent, sticking to her earlier decision. *It is not worth the risk.*

"There were remains of the black death in there," Nola continued, oblivious to the faerie's inner tirade and pointedly ignoring the glare. "That dark stuff you saw us with last time. It drains energy, life. But that was such a small dose that it will wear off before morning."

Filthy human magic. Kelty continued to glare at the girl as Nola returned to sweeping the bits of human flesh from the dirt floor. She took the dustpan to the far corner and shoved it into a bag with a grimace of revulsion. Then she turned back to Kelty.

"Don't look at me like that." Nola cringed and her voice cracked a little. Wiping at her eyes, she put the broom down and sank to the ground a few paces from the paralyzed faerie.

"I was forced into this, okay. It's a long story, but they did this to me." She worried her hands as she spoke, looking down at the ground. "They forced me to drink this gray stuff. I told them it didn't do anything to me, but they don't believe me, so now they keep me around by threatening my friends. I've been able to keep my, uh, abilities a secret from them so far, but I doubt that will last. Derek already suspects me."

The girl sniffed and wiped at her eyes again. Doing her best to remain skeptical, Kelty felt her resolve melting like Nola's tears. *Curse this human.*

Nola continued after a sigh. "I've played my part so that I can keep track of what they're doing. And hopefully to be close enough to find out a way to stop them. They're too rebellious and stupid for their own good. And that stuff is really dangerous. Well, now you've seen it." Lifting her gaze, she gave Kelty a weak smile that was more like a grimace.

The story had undercurrents of a powerlessness against this

group and their terrible magic. *Alone, like me.*

Then Kelty gave herself a mental shake. *Always a soft spot for the victim,* she chided herself. *It is what the blue one used to trap you before.*

If Nola could see the conflict in Kelty's face, she didn't let on. "That's why I asked for your help." Her voice got softer, taking on a more vulnerable tone. "I don't have enough magic to stop them. Only enough to see the magic in all the trees and plants—and you. I've seen the magic you have. I've watched you heal the trees and the plants. I can see it within you. If I have any hope of stopping them from using that magic to destroy everything around us, it's you."

Kelty closed her eyes as the verbal plea cut her to her core. The girl brought up the point she had refused to contemplate: She may be the only one around with the magic and the will to stop it.

Faerie that refuse to protect the life around them do not deserve to be called faerie.

Kelty sucked in a breath and let it go slowly. *Moon protect me from the curses I bring upon myself.* Without opening her eyes, she opened her mouth to answer. Nola sat silently, the air around her filling with hope and anticipation, desperation.

All that came out on Kelty's first attempt at words was a hoarse cough. She opened her eyes and turned to her back again as she tried to calm her breath. Nola regarded her with kind, worried eyes, hands hovering between them as if she would help Kelty if she could.

"Midday, midday tomorrow...at the tree," Kelty managed in a whisper that the girl strained forward to hear.

Nola smiled and nodded, relief apparent in her face. "All right." She stared uncertainly at Kelty, as if wondering if there was more the faerie had to say.

Kelty pointedly turned away, shame and despair at the future she may have lost with this one choice churning in her heart.

Taking the hint, Nola quietly rose and turned off the lantern, plunging the room into partial darkness, only a single beam of moonlight shining through the window.

Halfway to the door, Nola turned and paused, swinging back around. "Do you need any help—"

Kelty responded with a hiss.

Nola held up her hands and walked toward the door. "Okay. Okay. Until tomorrow." The door closed softly behind her.

Kelty turned her eyes to the sliver of moon just visible through the window. *Please let this be worth it.*

She lay there, helpless, as the moon climbed higher in the sky. Her pain eventually turned to anger. *These humans have gone too far. They will pay.*

Chapter 12

The next morning, Nola flew out of bed the instant after her alarm went off.

Today she would finally get some answers.

She hurried through showering and dressed in her usual jeans and T-shirt ensemble.

Once ready, she glanced at the time. 10:17. *Way too early.* And there wasn't much to do on a Sunday morning to distract her from her nerves.

Nola sat on the edge of her bed. Then she sighed and began pacing the small, sunny space between her bed and the desk that sat before her large window as she worried with the ends of her hair.

Her thoughts started to run in agitated circles. *I don't have any information to give the faerie.* Nola remained a member of the cloaks partially to observe and gather information that could be used to take them down. But what did she really have to show for that? A suspicion that someone else, these mysterious benefactors, were pulling the strings was not useful. She wasn't even sure of the specifics of the plans for the substances other than weapons and possibly enhancing human strength.

And my power isn't much of an advantage either. All I can do with that is observe, too.

With a sigh, Nola paused in her pacing to run one finger over the leaves of the plant she had rescued from her father's basement laboratory. It had been a castaway, brown and crumbling, not even fit for revival with the gray substance, in her father's mind. Now it sat in the sun on her desk, long green leaves spilling onto the floor.

She took a deep breath and cleared her mind of worry, focusing instead on the steady life energy of the plant. One of its thin leaves wound its way around her finger as she willed it. The small action brought a smile to her face.

The plant had been hopeless once, but it endured and now it had strength beyond reality.

Nola gently removed her finger from the leaf and retrieved her phone from the bed. She selected the number quickly and pressed it to her ear, heart pounding.

Cameron answered on the fourth ring. "Nola?"

"Uh, yeah. Hi. I was just wondering if maybe we could talk about last night." Nola cringed as the words came out.

There was a pause. Then he sighed. "I can't say much."

"Who will even know?" Nola asked.

He paused again. "They are everywhere, Nola."

Weird. Nola couldn't help a small shiver at his tone. "Who? These mysterious benefactors?"

"Yes. Look, Nola, it's really best if you just keep out of it. These are not people to be messed with. I'm not sure if they even are people, or at least we haven't seen them." He paused again. "I'll try to keep Derek's attention off of you as best I can, but that's hard when you question things."

Nola sat on the bed, mouth hanging open at his concern. *He is trying to keep Derek away from me?* "Um—" With effort, she gathered her thoughts and forged ahead. *Think about that later.*

This is your chance for answers.

"What do the benefactors want?" she asked. "Are they involved with the corporation? With Derek's father?"

"No," he answered. "They, uh..." He sighed in frustration. "They offered us a look into a world of magic if we made weapons for them."

You've got to be kidding me. Nola rose from the bed to pace again. *What does that even mean?*

"Why you?" she asked instead, knowing there wasn't much of a chance he would tell her the meaning of that statement, if he even knew in the first place.

"Something about human hands making human substances. It didn't make much sense, but Derek was really into it," he said, describing events that likely happened before Nola was forced into the group. "Look, Nola, you have to keep this to yourself, okay?"

Nola ignored his plea. None of this was making sense. She needed something she could use. "Do you know where Derek gets the gray stuff? Is it only from my father?"

"For now," he answered in a distracted voice. "Look, I have to go. Do not tell Derek or Adam, or even Jeanine, any of this."

"Okay, okay," Nola just managed to get in before he hung up. With a sigh, she fell back on her bed. *What on earth was he talking about?* Butterflies fluttered in her stomach at the implication that Cameron was trying to keep Derek off her case. *It will never last, though. Derek will get to him. Like when he held me down at Derek's orders when that stuff was forced down my throat.*

Nola forced her mind back to what he said about the benefactors. She turned his words over in her mind, but couldn't come up with much that made any sense. Except the beginnings of a plan.

She rose from the bed and made her way downstairs to the empty kitchen. *If their only supply is my father, perhaps I can create something that looks so much like it and replace the real stuff with it.*

There were plenty of holes in this plan, but it felt good to be doing something. *I will at least have something to offer the faerie when I ask her to help with this mess.*

Chapter 13

The dawn came again, as brilliant as ever. Kelty felt it through the trees and plants of the human wood. They sighed and opened themselves up to the light. And Kelty opened heavy eyelids in the darkness of her home tree.

She stewed for a minute in the cocoon of her blanket, as if the great life-giver had any right to shine so bright after the horrible events of last night. She had made it back to her home tree at some point in the early morning hours, unable to fly, dragging her feet the entire way. Her body remained stiff and still drained. She dug one toe into the soil and closed her eyes again, relaxing in the soothing sensation of the *ara* beneath the ground. Her power stirred in welcome.

My magic has replenished, at least.

After a few long minutes, Kelty forced her stiff muscles to cooperate as she rose into a sitting position. Running her fingers through her long silver hair, she stretched and flexed her wings. They shook a little, but it was a far cry from hanging dead on her back.

Standing was harder, but she made it over to the hollowed-out stone she kept water in on a wooden ledge a few paces away. About to dip a hand into the smooth surface, the reflection of the vial of black death, secure in its cage of reeds and magicked

71

rocks on a ledge a few feet above her head, gave her pause. Its mere existence taunted her. *Soon I will have answers.*

Pushing aside thoughts of what she would do in a few short hours, Kelty dipped her hands into the shallow water, splashing a liberal amount on her head and reaching with her power to coax the water to run along her body. It was a trick of water-users, the safety of her home tree giving her the courage to use it.

She cleansed off the human taint and the lingering memories of that awful, dark magic, but it could not erase her decision to put her magic, her faerie being, in danger to meet with the human girl.

There was a lingering thought in Kelty's mind that what she was to do today went against everything she was. *Humans do not see; they do not care. They turned their backs on magic. Their very existence is an offense to all living things.*

But so is this dark magic.

Kelty wrapped herself in the only thing she brought from Faerie, the long piece of woven cloth the color of the soil that grounded her. She infused the ends together over her front using a little coaxing of her magic, then pushed open her door to face the day.

Letting it gently swing shut behind her, she strode to a bush a few paces away. Blue wild berries grew on it in loose clusters, growing larger by the day under her care. She plucked a few and popped them into her mouth. Though finally strengthened with magic so as to contain enough energy for her to eat a few here and there during the day and survive, they could never compare to the richness of the fruit in Faerie.

As she chewed, Kelty examined the bush with one hand, infusing it with a little of her power where it looked weak.

Engrossed in her task, she startled as she turned her head and caught sight of the flower, an unearthly brightness next to the dull human plants.

It grew out of the soil right next to the base of her tree, five delicate yellow-white petals fanning out in the shape of a star.

A *lumin* flower.

They were native to Faerie. Kelty's heart beat faster. This flower was too close to her namesake to be a coincidence.

She sent her magic into the ground, and searched the sky and branches above, cursing herself for growing so comfortable in this land of outcasts that she hadn't done this as soon as she emerged from her home tree.

Kelty's body relaxed slightly as she found no trace of faerie anywhere near. Turning her attention back to the flower, she forced her feet forward. Kneeling, she reached forward with one tentative hand.

A warmth spread up her arm and through her body. Her magic warmed in response as the earthy smell enveloped her.

The watcher.

Her mind struggled to accept what her body already did, that this was meant to be a comfort. *He bears the mark of the Night, but his loyalties are unknown. And he will not even speak to me.*

Kelty sighed as she straightened, a nervous energy winding through her. *Who did he think he was to taunt her and then give her a precious gift?* A gift that meant he knew more than she was comfortable with.

There was no denying the message behind the star-shaped petals. He knew her secret over the affinities, and the name only a few trusted faeries called her. And he wanted her to know it.

Kelty's eyes still darted to the skies. She felt more exposed

73

and vulnerable than ever before. *How dare he do this to me.*

She took one more lingering look at the white flower before rising into the trees.

Once I am done with these humans, watcher, I will find you. And you will tell me what you think you know about me.

Chapter 14

Nola waited under the tree, fidgeting with the straps of her pack.

What if she doesn't show? What if she was hurt more than I thought last night? What if—

She caught a purple flash out of the corner of her eye. Peering up through the lush green leaves, she could just barely see the faerie. Then the leaves parted and Nola's eyes met a pair of startling silver ones.

Her color looked good, back to the rich purple from the pale almost gray color she turned last night. And her eyes had their sharpness back to them. The silver strands of her long hair fell to the side of the faerie's heart-shaped face as she cocked her head down at Nola, revealing a black, crescent moon-shaped tattoo on her right temple and the gentle curve of her ear. *Not pointed,* Nola thought in surprise.

The faerie's wings were collapsed to her back, hanging down the branch behind her, but from what Nola could see, the delicate, membranous wings almost seemed to shimmer in the light. *I hope I can see them up close sometime.*

Nola tried to solidify the vision in her mind, fingers itching to draw the faerie surrounded by the leaves as she was now.

She gave Kelty a small smile.

Kelty looked away into the trees, and the moment ended.

"You just going to stay up there, nameless forest spirit?" Nola asked.

"Yes." The faerie's voice came out as a light whisper, like the wind in the leaves. She kept her eyes on the distance.

Well, you couldn't expect her to trust you right away, not after what she's seen.

"I suppose I wouldn't want to be near me after last night either." Nola ran a hand through her hair and played with the ends as she spoke. "You're all right? It wore off?"

"Yes."

"Good." Nola smiled despite the fact Kelty wasn't looking at her. Removing her pack with one arm, she sat cross-legged on the ground. "Well, I'll tell you everything I know about the strange stuff." She paused and looked up again. "But I have some questions, too. And I'm hoping you can help me."

Slowly, Kelty turned her head to peer down at Nola again, her exotic eyes mesmerizing. "Speak."

Nola swallowed. "Are you a faerie of some kind?"

Those exotic eyes widened slightly. "Yes."

Nola gave her a pleased smile. "Do you have a name?"

Immediately, Kelty broke eye contact and leaned back. "No."

A small sigh escaped Nola and her shoulders slumped. "Nameless, it is then." She tried a different question. "What does that moon on your temple mean?"

Kelty unconsciously put a hand up to the mark. She hesitated before answering the question.

"It means I am of the Night," she responded slowly.

"The Night. As opposed to the Day?"

"Yes," the faerie answered in that breathy voice.

"Are there any others in the park?"

A slight pause. "No."

That's a lie, Nola thought, remembering the blue faerie outside the cabin the other night. *Unless maybe she doesn't know about him.*

"Have you always been here?" Nola moved on.

"Have you?" the faerie shot back, giving her a sharp look.

Nola grinned in amusement. *She really doesn't like answering questions. Yet, she hasn't asked any of her own.* "Yes. My house borders the fence on the far side of this park. I come here all the time."

The faerie closed her eyes in what looked like irritation, but then she spoke.

"I come from Faerie," she said tightly. "It is a world bordering this one." She opened her eyes again and narrowed them at Nola, as if daring her to ask more.

Nola grinned back at the grumpy faerie, eyebrows raised. "The faeries come from a place called Faerie?" she asked with skepticism.

Kelty merely blinked at her. "Yes."

These faeries certainly are different from the mischievous little things that I've read about, Nola thought in amusement. After first discovering the faerie, she checked out some books at the library. The lore on the subject certainly didn't describe the one before her.

Nola let the subject drop, sensing Kelty might become angered if she prodded. "Thank you. I'll tell you about the cloaks now."

Kelty merely stared down at her expectantly through narrowed eyes.

Bringing her knees to her chest, Nola started the tale, voice shaking a bit.

77

"My father works at a lab, it's a—it's a place of experiment-ing, of discovery and knowledge—gosh, I had this down in my head earlier. It's a place of science. It's the opposite of magic."

Kelty stiffened, placing a hand on the trunk of the tree as she leaned forward. "The opposite of magic is death."

"No, not death... It's the study of things you can see, things you can prove. It actually saves lives," Nola tried to explain.

"This science does not sound like a good replacement for magic."

Brows furrowed, Nola asked, "Replacement for magic?"

The faerie regarded her as if she were completely daft. "What the humans chose over magic long ago."

"You're saying we had magic once?"

The faerie raised her thin silver eyebrows. "The *ara*." She pronounced it *ah-rah*. At Nola's dubious expression, she elaborated with something like an eye roll. "The magic in the world around you."

Nola mulled it over for a second and slowly nodded in un-derstanding, thinking of the way the faerie seemed to glow the same as the life around her. "It is the same energy that's within you."

Kelty looked both pleased and disturbed at the same time. "You should not be able to see through my magic, human girl."

Nola stiffened at her tone. *Clearly the faeries have a problem with us humans.*

"I'll explain that in a second. Anyway, you don't really have to understand science. The cloaks really just mix substances with this gray stuff... So about a couple months ago, Dad got this strange substance. I don't know where he got it from. It always seemed to swirl, like of its own will. Almost like a gray cloud caught in a jar. And when applied to plants, they grew super fast. And so I stole some of it, hoping to help the park a little bit and also to keep it out of the hands of Derek and the corporation my dad works for. Derek's dad owns it. They are capable of doing some pretty horrible things with it, I'm sure. But now I'm more worried about these benefactors they keep mentioning—"

"This gray substance, is it like the black one? Are they made the same way?" Kelty leaned forward a little as she peered down with an intensity in her eyes.

"No," Nola answered. "The gray stuff is the basis of the black death, but I wasn't around when they mixed it. I don't know what else is in it. Do you know what's in it? I mean, if you got close enough the other day." It was Nola's turn to lean forward intently.

Kelty pressed her lips, that were a slightly darker purple than her skin, into a line. "I took the magic from the boy after he caused such destruction. It is like faerie magic, but it is also human. It drains the power I use on it."

Nola sighed. *So much for that.* Cameron's earlier words came back to her then. *Human hands making human substances...*

"Maybe it was made with something human and that's why your faerie magic won't work?" Nola raised her eyebrows, looking for any sign from Kelty that she was thinking in the right direction.

"Would there be iron in it?" Kelty asked, like the word left a bad taste in her mouth.

"Iron is your weakness?" *So I guess some parts of the stories are true.*

Kelty glared at her. "You were explaining how you can see through my magic."

Nola blinked. "Right. I uh—I never should have stolen it,

79

the gray stuff. Derek, the boy you saw the other day and at the cabin, he is my father's research assistant, and he found out. He used the opportunity to lure me out to the cabin and forced me to swallow the substance as an experiment. I didn't realize what happened to me until I walked outside and saw the light in the trees and plants and animals. Then I walked into the park and saw you."

Silver eyes regarded her intently. "The humans, what do they want with this dark magic?"

"I'm not entirely sure," Nola admitted. "They've talked about becoming stronger, gaining special powers of some kind. And lately they've been talking about these benefactors, so whatever they can get from them, money, whatever..." she trailed off, lamely.

"You are part of the group." The faerie gave her a confused look.

"They only keep me around so they'll know if I develop any side effects to the gray stuff. I'm there, but I'm hardly a part of the group," Nola argued.

"If no one sees you, you have to make yourself known."

Nola stared at her, mouth hanging open.

"Where does this gray stuff come from?" Kelty pressed on.

"I, uh, I don't know where my father gets it, but he keeps his stash in the basement and Derek steals from that—"

"That needs to be destroyed."

Nola shot her a look of annoyance. "I know. I tried mixing together some stuff that kind of looks like it. The color isn't exactly right, but I was hoping I could work on it and then switch them so Dad would think it spoiled or something. But that doesn't take care of where he got it from or even what it is in the first place."

"Ask him."

Nola shook her head. "I can't do that. He will never understand and I will probably be grounded for life for getting mixed up in this. And he will probably get fired if he confronts Derek. Or worse."

Kelty stared, a judging look on her face, but said nothing.

"Any idea what it is or where it came from?" Nola asked her. "It seems to be magical. Could it have come from Faerie?"

Kelty suddenly rose to her feet on the branch, wings fluttering in agitation.

"Do not speak of what you do not know," the faerie said through clenched teeth.

Nola rose to her feet as well. She held up her hands in a gesture of surrender. "Sorry. I just wanted to know, since you're magical and all—"

Kelty's head whipped to the side, an intensity taking over her expression.

"Later," she hissed quickly down at Nola and dove off the branch, disappearing into the foliage. Nola stared after her, mouth open in indignation.

Stupid, stupid, Nola chastised herself. *Now she might not want to talk again.* The question had been innocent, though she had to admit she could've phrased it so as not to imply the faerie was responsible for this.

"Later," Nola groaned. "That isn't specific at all." *Tomorrow is Monday. I will only have time to meet her after school. I need more answers now. I'm sick of waiting.*

With a sigh, she picked up her bag from the ground and started off in the direction Kelty had flown.

"I would not go any farther, human."

The voice froze Nola in place. An image of the blue one she

81

glimpsed the night before flashed before her eyes, causing her heart to skip a beat. But when she turned back slowly and looked up toward where the voice came from, a different faerie of green skin crouched on a branch above, partially concealed by leaves.

The voice was too low anyway, Nola thought in disappointment.

This new faerie's wings, as well as the long hair he wore tied into a braid, were a rich brown color. He wore a brown-beige cloth wrapped tight to his body in what Nola determined must be faerie fashion, though he left his chest bare. *I wish I could see if he has a moon tattoo on his temple like Nameless.*

He gave her a stern look, like a father warning a child not to do something or else.

Despite the fear in the forefront of her mind, the desperation got the better of Nola. "Why not?" she challenged the faerie. Regret flooded her in the next instant. *That sounded rude. Probably a dumb move.* But she refused to look away from the stern male's gaze. *What do I have to lose now, anyway?*

"That one is trouble," he said shortly, and then straightened and extended his wings. The spectacle caught Nola off guard as she marveled at the beauty. Nameless was delicate and gorgeous, where this faerie was rugged power.

She shook herself free at the last second before he took off. "Nameless?" Nola asked, then quickly clarified, "The purple one?"

The green faerie paused, a look of annoyance crossing his face. But just when she thought he wouldn't answer, he said, "No. The blue one."

And then he did fly off, quickly and quietly. In the next moment, Nola wondered if she imagined the whole thing.

No. I've seen three of them now. They definitely exist. I just have to figure out what their deal is, since they don't seem to like to give up information.

Flighty faeries, Nola grumbled internally as she continued on despite the warning.

Chapter 15

The traces of magic within the trees led Kelty back to her home tree, where Briar casually leaned against it. The darkness of him stood out against the brightness of the wood.

What does he want? Kelty hesitated in the cover of the leaves high above Briar.

Then the blue faerie lifted one delicate foot and slowly traced the petals of the *lumin* flower with his pointed toe.

Kelty's teeth clenched, wings twitching. *What does he want with my flower?*

She tucked her wings in tight and dropped through the branches to the ground below. Landing lightly a few paces away, she fixed Briar with a glare.

"Why have you come this time?" she demanded.

He didn't straighten from his casual position against her tree. "I warned you not to get involved with the humans." He lifted his dark eyebrows.

Kelty slowly rose from her crouched position and crossed her arms. "You did," she replied. "Now, why have you come?"

A frown pulled at his features and he lightly pushed off the tree to advance toward her. "How did the flower get here?"

Kelty backed up a step before forcing her legs to stand strong. "I cannot tell you that," she echoed his earlier words.

Briar stopped within arm's reach of her and smirked, mirroring her stiff stance. "It's a beautiful piece of Faerie." He threw a glance over his shoulder to the flower and back at her. "But this one shines too bright." His eyes hardened. "Too close to its namesake."

Kelty's heart began to pound. She worked to keep her face free of fear. *Namesake. He knew she was the Star.*

That made two faeries who knew her secret, while she knew barely anything about either of them.

"How do you know?" she asked in a hard voice.

"How do I know what?" he asked lightly.

Kelty pressed her lips into a thin line as she clenched her hands to keep from lashing out.

Abruptly, Briar turned and crossed the short distance to the flower. He ripped it from the ground with one hand; the petals immediately withered and crinkled in his grip, all moisture leaching from it to absorb into Briar's skin.

Eyes wide, Kelty moved forward only to halt in indecision. He was the one with the power here. And he knew it. She was the ultimate instrument of magic and especially vulnerable without the Night court to protect her in this world of unknown dangers.

Kelty trembled in fury as Briar crushed the flower with his fist, letting the bits fall to the ground.

"Be more careful with your secrets, Kelty of the Night," he said before disintegrating into the air.

"No." Kelty rushed forward too late. Grabbing her head in her hands, she let out a frustrated cry.

"Who was that?"

The voice nearly startled Kelty off the ground. She whirled, clutching her wings in tight to her back, magic at the ready, only to relax as Nola stepped into view.

Kelty turned away from the girl before she said something she would regret. She paced the short space in front of her tree home, mind a chaotic mess of fear and frustration.

"I didn't get to tell you that the cloaks are meeting tomorrow night. At the cabin, like usual," Nola said as if that excused her spying.

Kelty gave no outward sign she heard the girl.

"I suppose I won't get to know his name either?" Nola asked.

For all she sees, this one can be oblivious.

But after a few moments Kelty answered. "He is called Briar."

"That's a stupid name."

Kelty paused, one corner of her lips quirking up despite her mood. It was something her sister might say. The thought brought on a tightening in her chest.

"We should call him the blue death," Kelty muttered.

Nola's resulting laugh sent a shock of warmth through Kelty, her tension easing slightly.

"What's his problem? What did that flower do to him?" Nola sat cross-legged on the ground again, pack dropped at her side.

"It was a message." Kelty resumed her path back and forth. "A threat."

After it became clear she wasn't going to elaborate, Nola asked, "Think he's behind the gray stuff, the magic?"

Kelty spun toward her. "Why would you say that?"

Nola shrugged. "He said to stay away from the humans or something, didn't he?"

She may be right. Kelty turned away, dread spreading through her.

"I hardly know him. He may be responsible, and he may not be," she told Nola.

"How do you know him then?"

So many questions. Kelty closed her eyes against a burst of frustration and willed herself to calm. She opened them again to Nola gazing at her expectantly.

Shame brought heat to her face at the innocence in the girl's expression. She stepped back.

"That is a story for another day."

Nola's face fell, but she desperately threw another question at her. "Was he your boyfriend?"

Kelty crossed her arms and raised an inquisitive brow at Nola.

"Uh, someone who likes you more than a friend, a partner—"

A shudder went through Kelty at the word. "No. We are not partners." She turned away from the girl, anger warring with loneliness inside her.

"Sorry, sorry," Nola backtracked. "You don't need to tell me now, but what are we going to do about, well...all of it?"

Kelty looked sidelong at the girl. "Stay away from Briar." Without another word, she turned to her tree home.

Nola scrambled to her feet. "Oh, really? And what will you do?"

"You will see." Kelty pulled open her door.

"Is this where you live?" Nola scrambled to ask.

"Yes," Kelty said without looking back.

"Trust needs to go both ways, Nameless," Nola called after her as the door swung shut.

Guilt filled Kelty's mind at being so short with Nola, but she had not yet decided to trust her. *The less she knows, the better. Her human life is too fragile to be caught up in faerie conflicts. Especially this one.*

Chapter 16

Clenching her teeth, Nola stared at Kelty's beautiful door set into the bark of a tree. *I've never seen this before.* It was the same purple and silver color as the faerie with the shape of a silver moon in the center. Nola contemplated banging on it, but when she raised her hand to do it, she froze.

This will not help. She lowered her fist. Eyes wide in awe, she reached a finger to touch the wood. *I wonder how she gets the color.*

Then she blinked. *No. I will not stand out here admiring her house like an idiot.* Nola turned, stalking away through the trees.

I understand her hatred of humans, but I do not understand why she will not at least give me simple answers. I've given her plenty of answers—

Nola nearly screamed as a figure dropped out of the branches to land lightly in front of her. Hand over her heart, she stepped back a few feet.

The green faerie from before glared at her. He was taller than Kelty, his brown eyes even with Nola's.

She forced herself to stay put, though she wanted to back up more. She glanced around quickly, confirming they were alone. *It's a good thing we are still in the part people are not supposed to go,* she thought. *Or maybe it's not such a good thing,* she amended as she took in the look on the faerie's face.

He had warned her away before, but who knows what his motivations were for that. And she had no clue what his power was like. *I should've asked Nameless if faerie magic could be used against humans.*

"Why do you have so many questions, human girl who can see?" he asked in a commanding voice.

Nola's mouth dropped open. "I, uh—"

"Who do you answer to?"

"No one." To Nola's relief, that answer came out stronger. But that wasn't entirely true. "I mean, that group I am with—I don't really—I have kept my abilities and Nameless a secret and I will keep it that way."

He studied her impassively. "The one you call Nameless and the blue one, are they the only faeries you have seen?"

"Yes," Nola nodded.

He gave her another lingering look. Nola itched to ask him who he was, but something told her to keep her mouth shut.

After a moment, the faerie blinked, posture relaxing ever so slightly. He turned and quickly bent to retrieve something from behind the tree trunk they stood next to.

He held out a red spiral notebook to Nola. "Be more careful with this."

Eyes wide, Nola took it. A quick glance inside confirmed it to be hers, the colorful drawings she held so dear to her heart now safe within her grasp. "Where did you find this?"

"I took possession of it for study," he answered, as if that was completely normal. "It is important the knowledge in these pages remains a secret. She is important."

Nola glared at the faerie. *That green flash of light I saw.* "You stole it." She put the notebook in her pack while keeping both of her eyes trained on him.

A slow blink was his only reaction.

Fine. Nola caught herself before she rolled her eyes. Then she remembered his earlier words. *She is important.* "Who is Nameless?" Nola asked in awe.

A shadow came over his eyes and he leaned back. "If she has not told you, you may never know."

"And I suppose you won't tell me who you are?"

The green faerie studied her. "You are smart for a human."

"At least tell me you are on our side." *If Nameless and I are even on the same side.*

"If she will call you friend, then so will I."

More non-answers. Great.

"And we all at least agree that we hate the blue one?" she asked.

He pulled his lips back in an almost sneer, much like Nameless did. "He is trouble."

"Okay. So...what do we do now?"

"You will keep your secrets," he said as if it were obvious. Then he added with a stern look, "And ours." He turned from her.

"No, no, no." The outburst surprised even Nola, but she continued on as he looked over his shoulder. The temptation to study his rich brown wings was strong now that he was right in front of her, but she forced her eyes up to his and forged on. "I can help. I have been spying on Derek and the others even though it is the last thing I would ever want to do. Ever. I sit through their disgusting and terrifying experiments and I keep my mouth shut about all of this even though Derek threatens me. I want to take them down. I have stood by and watched for way too long. And I would say I have more claim to this wood than you do."

She was panting a little when she finished, half of her proud and satisfied and the other part terrified he would now turn her to dust with whatever faerie power he had.

Nola waited. The faerie continued to regard her with the same evaluating expression.

"So many passionate words. I may advocate for you when the time comes." He inclined his head in a slight bow and then leapt straight into the air, leaving Nola gaping up at him as he disappeared into the leafy canopy.

She breathed out a weary sigh, more unanswered questions swirling around in her head. The path before her was now more unclear than before.

I hate being so powerless. Always so powerless.

Chapter 17

Unable to sleep hours later, Kelty flew off into the night. The familiar darkness and the guiding light of the moon revived some of the energy drained by her guilt. *I was harsh with the girl. I let the blue one get to me.*

Running her fingers along the leaves and bark, Kelty absorbed the calm of the wood, listened to the rustle of animals in the brush and the clicking noises of the bugs, and let the cool air wash over her. Once the cabin came into view, she was centered and focused on her plan. The night was hers.

She perched in the crook of where a branch met its trunk above the cabin. This tree was the largest and most powerful, giving her a strong starting place to connect with the others. She closed her eyes and sent her magic deep down amongst the roots. They stirred, responding slowly to her magic touch. She increased the flow of energy, coaxing them to grow.

Life to a place of dead wood. Life to counter the death and destruction that goes on here. Despite their natural aversion to this place that housed dark magic, the green life obeyed Kelty's direction, spreading into the ground under the dirt floor of the cabin.

Dawn colored the sky when she opened her eyes again, task complete for now. She withdrew from the plant life. *So much more has to be given to the trees of this world.* Kelty straightened and stretched out stiff limbs, flicking her wings.

Her plan was ready to put into action when the humans met at the cabin that night. For now, she needed to rest.

Kelty cast a quick glance around to check for the presence of humans. The woods were nearly quiet at this hour, but a few visitors liked to walk the park early, using technology that she learned from their conversations was used to capture images. These ones were respectful to the woods, but had startled Kelty with their quiet presence numerous times.

In her weakened state, it would be easier not to bother camouflaging herself into the backdrop of the wood. Her keen eyes picking up nothing, Kelty swung off the branch and into the air above the pond so she could cross without the hindrance of the trees.

The earthy scent enveloped her just as she touched down on the far shore of the pond. Then a burst of energy alerted her to the watcher's presence.

This time she was prepared. Tapping into her last reserve of magic, she called the branches behind the green faerie to wrap around his feet, chest, and arms. She knew it likely wouldn't hold him, given he had a gift with the land like herself, but it would at least distract him.

The green faerie regarded her calmly, making no move to throw off his binds. Kelty's breath caught under his steady gaze. He was tall for a faerie; her head came up to his shoulder. Beneath those warm brown eyes was a straight nose and strong jaw, his brown hair pulled away from his face in a long braid. There was a lean strength to his body that suggested he did physical work in Faerie.

One of the Nym, as I once was. The Nym held the most

important job of tending to the balance of the *ara*.

Kelty had to give herself a mental shake. *You do not yet know if he can be trusted.* She squared her shoulders and crossed her arms, giving him a glare. "You are making things difficult, watcher. What is your purpose here?"

He stared for a second, studying her face with an intensity that made her want to squirm. "To watch," he finally answered in his rich, smooth voice.

This only gets more maddening. Kelty didn't bother to hide her sigh of frustration. "You've done more than that," she accused.

He opened his mouth to reply, but she cut him off. "Why would you be watching an outcast? Who sent you?" she demanded.

Indecision flickered in his brown eyes. "I am not to say. But it is someone close to you."

His words matched her suspicions, yet not his actions.

"If that were true, you would be doing more than merely watching. And you would not have to be so secretive," Kelty challenged.

His face took on a pained expression, but he said nothing. His silence stoked the storm of emotions building inside Kelty. The words that taunted her into getting involved in human conflicts, the image of the *lumin* flower as it withered and died in Briar's hands. Her heart hardened against this faerie who claimed to be on her side.

"Why did you bring the flower?" she asked in a low voice.

"It was a gift," he said.

"And a message?"

Indecision flickered in his eyes. *Maybe he does not know the trouble the flower has caused,* Kelty thought. *Maybe he will explain himself.*

But the watcher didn't answer, looking at a loss for words.

Frustration threatened to swallow Kelty. *I am tired of all this. So tired.*

"You will tell no one," she warned him. "And you will leave my wood."

His eyes widened. Kelty released the branches entwined around him and turned her back, flying off into the trees.

If he is a true friend, he will follow. He will explain. And he will tell me the truth.

When Kelty made it back to her home tree, she was still alone.

* * *

That night, Kelty returned to the large tree above the cabin to wait for the humans. The darkness failed to soothe the ache in her chest this time.

With rest had come clarity. *I don't know why I sent him away,* she lamented, leaning back and closing her eyes. And she didn't know why it bothered her so much that she did.

A flare of energy formed to her right. Eyes snapping open, she bolted up into a crouch on the branch, heart in her throat. The magic brought with it a coolness and the smell of rain.

Kelty tensed as Briar materialized among the leaves not far from her perch, delicately balanced on the branch.

"Someone's delighted to see me," he said dryly.

"I had hoped it would be anyone other than you." Kelty worked to keep her voice steady, though her magic roiled within her at his proximity. "What else have you come to take from me?"

She expected a snarky reply, but the smirk slipped from his face. "I will keep your secret," he said quietly.

She believed him, but only because it made sense for him to hold this over her. *I will have to find a way to stop him before he sees an opportunity to give me up as the Star.* For now, she needed to figure out what his deal was with the humans. "Why did you really warn me away from the humans?" she demanded. "I would appreciate an answer this time."

Briar gave her a short laugh at that. "Because you have a fondness for danger."

Kelty's mouth dropped open at the implication he had just been playing with her. Before she could get control of herself, she lunged through the leaves toward him, stopping when she stood with her face directly in his. To his credit, he only leaned back slightly, a flicker of doubt crossing his delicate features for just a second before he masked it with lofty confidence.

"You think you know me," she challenged.

"Well, you are here," he threw back at her.

Kelty's heart pounded and her eyes narrowed at the audacity, at being faced with the truth. *You have crossed the wrong faerie, blue one. Once I think of a way out of this, you're mine.*

Suddenly aware at how close they were, Kelty backed away, gracefully stepping back to her original perch while keeping her eyes on Briar. "You still haven't told me why you're here," she said through her teeth.

"I have a job to do."

"You are working for the humans?" She pinned him with her eyes, a smirk of her own tugging at her mouth at his wince.

"Guess again," he said in a voice of forced lightness.

Kelty's jaw tightened. *Fine. I will play the game.* "The humans are working for you."

"Closer."

Then she voiced the fears that had been in her mind since she first saw Briar in the human world. "There are more faeries. Other outcasts are involved in this."

He said nothing, but there was truth in his dark blue eyes. Kelty ripped her gaze away. *Shame upon our kind. Have these outcasts lost sight of their purpose?*

She glanced at the cabin. Still quiet.

"What does any of this have to do with me?" she asked, fixing her gaze on the pond instead of his traitorous face.

"Now you are in the way," Briar answered in an odd voice. Kelty turned to see a sort of excited glint in his eye, but she had no time to contemplate it.

The snap of twigs below accompanied by the rustle of leaves alerted her to the arrival of the humans. They emerged from the cover of the trees in one large group. She picked out Nola toward the back next to the tall boy, whose blond hair was peeking out from beneath his hood. Derek unlocked the door. The others followed in single file. Nola threw a quick glance around the treetops before entering the cabin, but showed no sign she spotted either faerie.

Body tense, Kelty sized up Briar. He turned and did the same to her. They were in a different world now, and, given their very brief history, neither knew what the other intended to do.

Briar broke the silence. "I suppose you have some brilliant plan to carry out with the small female?" He cocked his head to the side, eyes glinting. "She is different than the others."

Something about the way he said *different* irked Kelty. *This ends now.*

"Guess again," she taunted.

Keeping his gaze, Kelty extended her left hand to the side,

97

palm up. Gathering her magic, she sent it into the tree at her feet and up through the roots directly under the cabin. Then she closed her fist. The shrieks below told her the roots had successfully burst through the dirt floor to grab at the humans. She gave Briar a little smirk as they fled the cabin.

Briar leaned forward as if he might do something, reaching up to steady himself by grabbing the branch above. But the whole spectacle happened too quickly for him to react.

He turned to her with anger marring his pretty face.

Kelty tensed, but forced herself to glare back at him. *I can play games, too.*

"You can have tonight. I will have the next one," Briar promised in a dark voice, but then the smirk flashed back across his face before he spread his wings and took to the sky, almost immediately blending in with the darkness.

Trying to ignore the chill that spread through her at his words, Kelty took off in the opposite direction. *One day I will be free of him,* she tried to convince herself.

Chapter 18

There was a sort of excitement in the air of the stuffy, dimly lit cabin. Nola's eyes darted between the faces of the cloaks. *What has gotten into them? What did they do?*

"Our benefactors actually think the red power has potential," Derek said, his face taking on that slightly manic expression he got when he was playing with fire. "We are one step closer."

Adam and Jeanine both stood slightly taller at the news. Cameron's eyes darted to Nola before he hastily looked away again. Nola made a point to study Jeanine's impractical wedge heels peeking out from the edges of her cloak.

To do what exactly? Nola itched to say, but she kept her mouth closed. *He's almost...happy. Maybe he will let something else slip—*

A sudden burst of energy filled the ground below them. Glowing lines stirred in the soil. *The roots,* Nola just had time to think before they burst from the dirt floor. She jumped back with a cry as one nearly tangled in her hair and another coiled around her feet. Jeanine screamed bloody murder, while Adam and Derek dove for the door. Cameron kicked at the roots twining their way around Jeanine's legs. Nola ducked out of the cabin just ahead of them.

Once outside, Jeanine pushed Cameron's arms away and took

off, awkwardly tottering on her heels. Cameron gave Nola a questioning look. She gave him a shrug back and waved him away toward the others, hoping he would take the hint and let her go in the opposite direction in peace.

Cameron nodded in understanding and started toward the others. Nola broke into a jog in the direction of home, knowing she should play the part of terrified human and wanting to be as far away from Derek as possible.

It took a while for Nola's heartbeat to slow. *A warning would have been nice, Nameless.* There was something about roots bursting through the ground to tangle at her feet that was truly terrifying, even though she knew who was behind it. But a small smile found its way to her lips as she thought of their terrified faces.

Then the smile slipped as Nola shook her head. *It definitely scared them, but was it the right move? It may just have scared them away from the cabin. I would've told her that if she listened.*

She made her way to the part of the wood that ran behind her backyard. Lost in thought, she almost missed the dark figure that waited for her at her back fence.

"You did this," Derek said, face almost invisible in the darkness.

No, no, no. Nola backed up a step at his tone, heart in her throat.

"I can't do anything like that," she struggled to keep her voice steady.

"When did you become such as accomplished liar?" He stepped menacingly towards her. "Who else could have done that? There is no one else that even has the possibility of having that kind of power. It was like the gray power times ten."

Definitely the wrong move, Nameless, Nola thought frantically.

What came out of her mouth next surprised her. "You really think that we were the only ones in those woods?"

Once the words were out, she cringed internally. *Why did I just admit that? Now he will think I am crazy.*

But Derek paused. "You think something else did this?" he asked, as if she actually had a good point.

"Perhaps," Nola said shortly. *Is he actually going to believe this? Has he seen the faeries?*

Derek was silent another moment. "I will look into it," he said. Without another word, he walked off into the night, black cloak blending in with the darkness.

Nola stared in shock at the space where he had been, her whole body starting to shake. *He knows more than he lets on. This is bad.*

"Impressive," a different, more sultry voice drifted to her through the darkness. "You have mastered the art of misdirection."

What now? Too tired to be quite as startled this time, Nola turned toward the semi-familiar voice.

She looked straight into the face of the blue one, the one called Briar. The one that was supposedly trouble.

He hung from a branch with one arm as if the position was totally comfortable for him. He glowed brighter than the plant life around him, almost like a giant firefly. Though probably about an inch shorter than Nola, his head was even with hers in this position.

Oh, no. I have no idea what this one is capable of.

Aloud, Nola answered, "Blue faerie." It came out a little cockier than she felt.

Briar dropped to the ground. He gave her a curious look as he crossed his arms and leaned sideways against the tree he had been hanging from.

"Why are you with them?" he asked.

Nola's mouth dropped open and all she could muster was a very unintelligent, "Um."

"I ask because you are not like them," Briar explained.

Despite who he was, Nola couldn't help but feel touched. "They threatened my friends if I didn't participate. They forced me to swallow a magic substance and still feel like they need to watch me for the effects. Derek is convinced I am hiding something."

Nola clamped her mouth shut. *Why did I just tell him my secret?*

"So that is how you can see," he mused. "They have cruelly mistreated you, human girl. Next time will be more pleasant." His lips curved into a charming smile.

The decree was absurd enough that she scoffed at him. "I wish."

Briar fanned out his wings then, a darkness against the glow of the trees, and took a step toward her. Nola sucked in an awed breath. "I will see that it is done," he said.

And with that, he rose into the sky and disappeared into the dark outline of the wood.

Faeries are not very good at goodbyes, Nola thought in shock as she turned toward her house.

That night, she sat up in bed, wired despite barely being able to keep her eyes open. Briar's words ran through her mind on an endless loop.

The supposed enemy was the only one that gave me answers, that made me feel seen.

Chapter 19

Kelty sat alone, almost concealed by the tall grass she had nurtured back to a healthy, yellow-green color moments before. The grass whispered in the gentle wind. The sun beat down on her, and for once she didn't care. Two days had passed. The cabin remained quiet, still giving off a dark energy, but Kelty worked to grow the roots and plants up within the structure, overwhelming the place with life to chase out the death. Nola was strangely absent from the wood, as was Briar. And the watcher apparently obeyed the order she hadn't meant.

It was almost like time had turned back to before Derek and the dark magic, before Nola's plea for help. It was something Kelty wished for in moments of frustration. She imagined solace and the ability to focus on what really mattered: getting back home.

This return to the way things were should have been peaceful, a respite. Instead, an emptiness plagued Kelty. *Why do I feel like I have failed?*

She closed her eyes with a sigh, digging her toes into the soil, its scent intensifying. And then a presence flared behind her.

Kelty rose to her feet and whipped around in one motion, heart in her throat.

The watcher stood, one hand resting on the trunk of the tree next to him, dark brown eyes intense, expression guarded. He said nothing.

Heart hammering in her chest, Kelty stared back, not knowing how to make words out of the mess in her head. She opened her mouth once and then closed it. Swallowing, she tried again. "You've returned."

Her cheeks heated immediately. *Moon and stars,* she cursed internally. *Of all the things to say.*

But his mouth curved into a small smile. "Do I have permission to stay for a short while?"

Kelty's heart fluttered as she nodded. "My apologies for ordering you away. I—I don't understand why you are here in the first place." She crossed her arms over her middle to keep from fidgeting and studied the distant sky without really seeing it.

"Kye of the Night sent me."

At his blunt answer, she jerked her focus back to him. "Mother sent you," she repeated in disbelief. Hope and joy ran through her at the name, only to be replaced by disbelief.

"How do I know you speak the truth?" she demanded.

His eyebrows knit together as he thought. "The Day grow restless in Faerie. A group of rebels threatens the rule." He shifted on his feet and folded his arms across his bare chest, wings giving a little twitch. "It is certainly convenient for them to have the heir of the Night banished." Then his gaze drifted up to meet hers.

Kelty's eyes widened at the unexpected information. *The Day. It must be true that they hired Briar to trick me. Though it must've been at a great price for him to agree knowing he would be banished as well. Unless they betrayed him.* Her thoughts ran in circles with the possibilities, frustration rising at all the unanswered questions she still had. With a sigh, Kelty pushed them aside.

"That did not answer my question," she told the green faerie before her.

He blinked. "I was sent to watch, and ordered not to communicate with you. I do not know how to prove myself."

"Sent to watch? That is all?" Kelty tried to keep her face from revealing the pain in her heart. *What purpose could that serve? What if they don't want me back?*

"Have you told them of my involvement with the humans?" Kelty fired another question at him before he could answer.

"I have not," he assured her in a rushed voice, a warmth in his eyes. "It was the right thing to do."

An answering warmth started in her core at his words, but her tension eased only slightly. His approval wouldn't provide her any help.

"I'm still waiting for proof," Kelty reminded him as she began to pace. He remained just inside the trees, a distance between them.

"They have not forgotten." His soft words stopped Kelty in her tracks. "They are being careful."

They have not forgotten. Tears of joy pricked at the back of her eyes, but she swallowed past the lump in her throat and turned back to him, searching for a lie.

His eyes were kind, his expression open. She could find no trace of deceit. The last bit of animosity she held toward this faerie melted away.

"Why did you reveal yourself against orders?" she asked quietly, holding his gaze.

"They are not so different from us, the humans," he replied in an even tone.

Kelty dropped his gaze, disappointment at his words shocking her. *What did I want him to say?*

"You are a strange faerie," she said aloud.

"As are you."

She sighed and looked up at him again, deciding to take a chance. *I need someone on my side.*

"Briar knows of my abilities," Kelty tested him, voice slightly shaky.

He inclined his head silently, the expression in his eyes hardening. *So he knows of the blue one.*

"He destroyed the *lumin* flower," Kelty went on. "He said I should be more careful with my secrets."

Guilt flashed across the green faerie's face. "My apologies, Star. I will be more careful."

Without another word, he grasped the stone at his throat and was gone in a burst of light.

Kelty blinked at the space where he had been, not sure what to think.

The green faerie's intentions were still unclear. He hadn't even offered his name. But he had come back despite her ordering him away. And his words confirmed her family was trying to clear her name. A warmth settled into Kelty's chest. *I may still be able to go back home. I hope it is not too late.*

Chapter 20

Nola stepped foot in the park for the first time in two days. The calm of the life energy within the plants and soil washed over her as she walked. She inhaled, breathing in the peace of the wood, the place she always loved, but that Nameless nurtured to a level beyond its prior beauty.

I missed this. Nola walked close to the trees and bushes to one side to avoid others on the path, occasionally reaching out a hand to run her fingers over the spring leaves.

Schoolwork kept her busy the past days, as well as playing along like she was spooked from the faerie's stunt at the cabin. She also spent most of last night planning a way to get into the basement to swap out the gray substance with the fakes she made. Now, she needed input from the one who had more stake in this, more to lose if the plan failed and Nola lost her connection to the cloaks or worse.

After a long while, she tracked the trail of purple energy to a shadowy part of the wood. The faerie stood at the base of a tree that was split in half, as if giant hands had taken each side and wrenched it apart. Each half of the tree was leaning almost to the ground. *Must've been lightning.* Nola paused a good distance away, eager to see if the faerie was capable of healing the tree.

Instead, those silver eyes shifted to find her in the shadows.

Nola sighed and walked forward.

"The cloaks think I was the one that pulled that stunt at the cabin," Nola called. "Or at least had something to do with it. They think there is some force or creature out here now and also that the cabin is cursed. We will be meeting elsewhere now, so as not to disturb the cursed energy."

Derek acted strange in school after that night. Nola was pleasantly surprised that he didn't utter a word to her about her supposed abilities and lies. *Either Briar was true to his word or there is something really strange going on that is bigger than we think. Or both.*

The faerie peered at her. "They think you are powerful," she said, as if the benefits of that were obvious.

Nola crossed her arms. "They are less likely to let me in on their secrets now. And they might take the magic elsewhere."

Kelty sighed. "What do you wish me to do?" She cocked her head challengingly at Nola.

"We need more of a plan," Nola said. "I can switch out the gray stuff with the stuff I made, but I don't think that will really do much good. Derek will freak out if their supply stops. And I don't even want to think about what these benefactors are like."

The faerie's gaze drifted back to the split tree. "We may not be enough," she said quietly. Her voice, like the whisper of leaves, had a chilling effect. "This may claim your life. And I am too close to this as it is."

"What's that supposed to mean?" Nola placed a hand on her hip as she glared at the faerie. "You may be the only one that can stop this, and I can help you."

"It is not so simple," Kelty answered.

Nola waited with raised eyebrows.

"I have been cast out of Faerie. The only way I can see to earn my way back is to keep my magic alive and pure, to restore this wood, and to keep out of human messes."

No, no, no. I thought we were past this part. Where did these second thoughts come from? "And how do you stay pure?" She tried to have patience.

"Exposure to humans drains our magic." She gave Nola a pointed look.

Oh, that changes things. "How does that happen?"

Kelty paused. "They seem to repel it. I do not know for sure, but the faerie will notice if I am weakened. I will not be allowed to return."

"Well, you've done a great job of staying out of human messes," Nola said dryly. "And you've been around me. Seems like the damage is already done. Why not take the humans down and then you never have to see them again?"

Kelty glared at her, at a loss for an answer.

"You have the chance to save lives, why not take it?" Nola asked. "You were important in Faerie, right?"

The faerie narrowed suspicious eyes at her. "How did you know that?"

"I met a green faerie," Nola admitted, eyes dropping to the bed of leaves beneath her feet. She pushed some around with the toe of her sneaker.

"What else did you discuss with this green faerie?" Kelty asked in a hard voice.

Nola dared a peek up at Kelty, who now inspected the tree on the farther side, fingers running carefully over the splintered wood. *She doesn't look surprised.* "Who is he?" she said instead.

"Only a watcher."

"He would not tell you his name either?" *I wonder if all faeries*

109

are like this.

Kelty looked at her then. "It may be dangerous for his name to be associated with mine."

"Why would that matter here? Who's going to know?"

"He still lives in Faerie," she said, as if that explained it.

Nola sighed. *It's like pulling teeth.* She slipped her arms from the straps of her pack and set it on the ground, lowering herself to sit crossed-legged beside it. "Well whoever you were in Faerie, I guess doesn't matter here, right? You can choose who you want to become now. Why not become the true guardian of the wood? Why is it not that simple?" Nola implored the faerie. "What if the faerie never welcome you back and you spend your life here waiting and not taking action?"

The faerie's eyes suddenly flashed, pinning her with a glare as the leaves around them rustled in warning.

No, no, no, too far. "I mean—" Nola tried to backpedal.

Kelty broke eye contact and the leaves quieted. Nola's guilt tripled at the pain that replaced the anger in the faerie's expression. *Maybe I am asking too much of her. She's lost her family. This isn't her home.*

"I will do what is necessary to cure the wood of the scourge brought on by Briar, nothing more," Kelty repeated, a dark sadness coloring her words. "And then I will go home," she added with more vehemence.

Nola swallowed and nodded. "Right. Thank you, Nameless."

A tension-filled silence fell over them. Leaning over, Kelty placed both of her hands in the center of the tree, one palm on each side of the split. Magic light flowed from her into the tree, a radiant, glowing warmth.

Mesmerized by the light that spread through both halves of the tree, Nola jumped when the faerie spoke. "What did you speak of with the green faerie?"

"What? Oh, he stole my notebook. He gave it back with a warning, I guess, not to mess things up for you. You really don't know who he is?"

A strange look passed over the faerie's face, though she remained focused on the tree. The light almost filled the split trunk halves. "He did that?"

"Yes, Nameless. He must like you at least a little to be talking to a human, right?"

Kelty said nothing, but her expression relaxed a bit.

Then she stepped abruptly back from the tree. Nola scrambled backwards at the burst of energy, the warmth emanating from it. She shielded her eyes from the light with her forearm, but couldn't look away.

Arms out to her sides, palms up, Kelty slowly brought them up as the halves of the tree rose to join again in the middle, knitting together rapidly. When Kelty's hands met above her head, the warm light dissipated. The tree stood whole again.

Nola lowered her arm, jaw hanging open. The whole spectacle was over in a matter of seconds. *She's so powerful. How on earth did the cloaks create a magic that she can't defeat?*

Kelty's voice broke into her thoughts. "He just revealed himself to me. My mother sent him," she said as if she hadn't just put a living tree back together.

What? Nola shook her head. *Oh, the green one.*

"To do what? Why would she send him?" Nola seized on the chance for information. She stood, dusting the leaves off her jeans.

Kelty began to wander down the path as she answered, as if seeking a distraction from the topic. "To watch."

"You faeries like to do a lot of watching and waiting," Nola said as she scrambled to grab her pack and follow.

"And you humans are prone to rash action," Kelty shot back.

Nola laughed. "I suppose that is true." The faerie glanced back at her in surprise. The glint of the sunlight on her silver wings caught Nola's attention. She ran her eyes over them, memorizing details as if she might draw them later. They were collapsed flat on the faerie's back, the bigger top section tucking over the bottom in folds like a paper fan, but Nola could still see the veins of a slightly darker silver creating scales just like that of a butterfly.

"Do all faeries have wings?" Nola blurted out.

Kelty gave Nola a surprised look, self-consciously turning toward her so that her back faced the wood. "Of course."

Nola held up one hand. "I won't touch them or anything. Just looking. They're gorgeous."

Kelty eyed her warily. "A faerie's wings are their greatest strength, but also their greatest weakness."

"Why?"

"Flying is a great advantage, yet the wing itself is susceptible to injury."

"Good to know," Nola nodded, giving the faerie a smile. "Not so hard, is it?"

"What?"

"Talking to me."

"I suppose not," Kelty admitted. "But never speak of such things to others."

Nola placed her hand over her heart. "You have my word, Nameless."

The faerie looked curiously at the gesture and then continued on down the path.

"Do all faeries have magic?" Nola prodded again.

"We are born with it, though some more than others. And all have different affinities."

"What is yours?"

Kelty hesitated before she answered. "I have a gift with the land, the growing things of the world." Her tone sounded a little off, like she was leaving something out. Nola moved on, though.

I'm finally getting somewhere. Best not to prod too close to her secrets. She can keep some for now if it makes her feel better. After all, I am keeping one as well.

Butterflies danced in her stomach as she thought of Briar and how he had called Derek off of her, when even Cameron could not. *Nameless will not appreciate hearing that. At least not now, not before I can get some information out of him.* The plan was only half formed in Nola's mind, but she was sick of waiting and inaction; she needed this.

But that didn't mean she was naive enough to think she was prepared.

"What is Briar's?" Nola asked, trying to sound innocent.

"Water." A picture of a mermaid flashed through Nola's head. But, no, the blue faerie was nothing like that. *I would like to see him in action, though.*

"Do faeries fight with this magic?"

"Yes, though not as frequently as humans fight."

They came to a stop as the crunching of gravel and human voices drifted to them from not far off.

Nola worried her lip. "You said you would help," she reminded the faerie in a hushed voice. "What is it you think we should do now?"

Kelty let out a hiss, causing the girl to jump, though it didn't appear to be directed at her. "The blue one and those he is working with will need to be dealt with, though removing the source—"

"Those he works with?" Nola's broke in louder than she intended. She then lowered her voice at Kelty's glare. "You know who they are? You know who the benefactors are?"

"Only that they are faerie. Most likely outcasts."

Nola raised her eyebrows. "How do they get here anyway, the outcasts?"

"The rulers of the Day and Night courts possess the magic to travel the path to Earth. They bring the outcasts and leave them without the magic to return."

"And these rulers wouldn't be behind the magic?"

Kelty sighed. "They have more important matters to deal with in Faerie. And they...dislike humans."

Right. Faeries hate us.

"You didn't think I might want to know this, Nameless?"

"I will take care of them."

Nola heaved a sigh. "That's not the point. We don't have a chance if we don't work together on this."

The faerie studied her for a moment. "It would be best to find the source first. We remove that and they are powerless. Perhaps you can use your newfound power to convince the humans to give up their secrets."

"Perhaps you can discover what these faeries want with human teenagers and messed-up magic," Nola retorted. "And see if the green one will help us. Bat your eyelashes at him or something."

"What?" the faerie asked, looking genuinely confused.

"Nevermind. Meet tomorrow afternoon at your tree?"

Kelty gave her a nod. In one swift movement, she opened her wings and launched into the air.

Well, at least that was somewhat of a goodbye.

Chapter 21

Kelty flew towards her home tree with purpose, her conversation with Nola sparking something inside of her, something a lot like guilt. The humans created the magic, but it was likely these faeries were the ones ordering them to do it, and were possibly involved with its creation. She had to figure out what it was they wanted. And the dark magic still hidden in her home might just be the key.

She had avoided dealing with the black death any more than making sure it remained bound within its magical cage. Kelty feared the draining of her power, especially now that she had confirmation her family was working to bring her home. But Nola was right, she may be the only one who could figure it out.

As she neared her home tree, the air thickened until a moisture coated her wings. *Think of him and he shall appear.*

Weaving through the trees, she dropped down beside Briar, but he was too fast, ducking nimbly out of her way. She had hoped to get in an unfaerie-like punch or a kick at him to throw him off, but at least he was now farther from her home. Briar turned to regard her with a smirk as she moved to stand in front of her door, arms crossed.

"Almost," he said.

"Leave," the word sprang instantly from her lips. Then

she cringed inwardly. *Moon above, I'm supposed to be getting information from him.*

Luckily, he didn't have a talent for obeying. "I need the magic back, Kelty."

"Don't call me that," she snapped. "What are you talking about?"

"The human leader lost a vial of a dark magic in this wood the other day. He said a tree branch fell on him and he must have dropped it then. How coincidental."

"What do they need it for?" Kelty ignored the demand. "What could faeries possibly want with a magic that is the opposite of life?"

His eyebrows rose and he cocked his head to the side. "You really think I am going to tell you?"

She glared. "Why do you want it back? You can just make more."

"I cannot make more," he said. "The humans can, but they have their limits." He stepped forward, hand extended, palm up.

The humans need to make it. It echoed what Nola had said the first time they spoke under the message tree. Kelty's mind raced. She needed to keep him talking.

"The Day planning on using it to terrorize their subjects?" she asked nastily.

"I cannot tell you that."

An uneasiness grew in the pit of her stomach at the answer that was not an outright no. "Whatever the conflict, this magic is not the answer."

"I know."

She gave him an incredulous stare. "Then why are you with them?"

Briar was quiet for a moment. "Some of us don't get to choose."

The pieces started clicking together in Kelty's mind. *They have some sort of hold over him. Like he has a hold over me.*

"They wanted me out of Faerie so the Day could carry out whatever it is they are planning," she said aloud, studying Briar's face for a reaction.

A slight frown creased his brow at her words.

I am right. The Day know I am the Star. He did this for them. I may never be welcomed back to Faerie. The rulers of the Day will make sure my name cannot be cleared. My secret was my downfall after all.

The moisture in the air around them grew to the point where beads of water settled onto their skin. *He is preventing our words from being heard.* Kelty's heart pounded as Briar took a step forward and then another until he was standing directly in front of her. Every instinct within her screamed to either run or attack. Neither would do her any good.

She clenched her fists and reigned her magic in tightly, forcing herself to stay still as Briar leaned over to whisper in her ear. "No. I wanted you here so that you could stop them."

Kelty's mouth dropped open, a dull roar sounding in her ears. She was barely aware of Briar's movements as he reached behind her to push open the door, magical protections dissolving under the moisture seeping into it. A second later, he whipped his arm back, the vial, wrapped in its cage of magicked stones, in his hand. The stream of water he used to retrieve it splashed to the ground. Without another word, Briar vaulted into the air.

Recovering, Kelty flew after him, crashing up through the treetops the way he had. But once she was in the sky, there was no trace of him to follow.

He brought me here as a weapon. Kelty tucked in her wings and let herself drop to the ground, sinking to her knees once she touched down. *He had me banished for this.* She looked down at her shaking hands as fury spread through her. And *I played right into his hands.*

Chapter 22

"There's something you should see before everything goes down on Monday. Meet me right behind the trees in your backyard."

Those had been Cameron's mumbled words to Nola at school that morning. *What could he possibly have to show me?* Nola's stomach was alive with butterflies as she tried to casually walk across her back lawn as if she was just going for a stroll. *It can't be anything good. But I guess my supposed influence is working on somebody. Whatever it is might change the game for us.*

There had been a time when she would've been alive with giddy excitement over a secret meeting with Cameron. His gorgeous features had been the subject of many drawings in her notepad. Now the fluttering in her stomach was mostly due to the nature of this meeting. *How things have changed in such a short time.*

If Nola hadn't been expecting him, the sight of his tall, cloaked figure out of the corner of her eye would've scared her close to death. *I'm getting way too comfortable with creepy cloaked figures.*

"Cameron?" she asked, since his face was still concealed. Her heart froze for a second, wondering if someone else would be under the hood, a perfect trap. But the figure removed his hood to reveal Cameron's blond locks.

"Nola," he nodded stiffly at her.

Weird, she thought about the formal gesture.

"What did you want to show me?" Nola asked, a little suspiciously. Though he was much safer than Derek, he was acting quite strange.

Cameron didn't say anything. Instead he closed the distance between them, looked into her eyes, and in one fluid motion leaned in to press his lips against hers. Frozen in shock, Nola didn't return the kiss. It was a moment she had dreamed about, and it was all wrong. In fact, she wanted to lean back and break it.

It was over quickly, and Cameron's lips made their way to her ear. "Turn to your right and keeping walking straight," he whispered. As articulate as ever, Nola only stared as he flipped his hood back up and strode out of the trees.

What just happened? Nola's mind spun as she pressed her fingers to her lips. Her first kiss, and it had only been a distraction. It came from someone who held her down as the substance was forced down her throat. It meant nothing.

Well, not nothing. She swallowed down the shock and self-pity. *I need to find what he wants me to see.*

Per instructions, she turned to her right and started to walk. The overgrown bushes made it difficult to stay on a straight path, but she tried her hardest. Eventually, she started to try willing the plants to move for her. Maybe it was her imagination, but she thought she felt the green life giving way to her more readily.

The day turned out to be a hot one, and before long, Nola's mouth and throat were dry. *What would he want me to see behind my own house anyway? I know these woods like the back of my hand.* But Nola had to admit that now she no longer played among the trees like she had in her younger days.

"Human girl." The voice startled Nola out of her thoughts.

She turned to see Briar crouched on a branch just above her. Up close and in the sunlight, he was a breathtaking sight, blue skin and black wings glinting. His long hair was swept back, revealing the tattoo of a sun on his temple. Nola traced the lines of the crude design with her eyes.

"Be careful," he said.

"Of what?"

He dropped from the tree and gestured behind her. Nola turned as the faerie pulled back the leaves with one arm. His closeness distracted her as the fresh scent of rain and spring washed over her.

Then the power slammed into her like a wall. She jerked her gaze to the direction of his arm.

There was no mistaking what the gray puddle on the ground was.

The gray substance. *This is the source.*

She glanced sideways at Briar, summoning her courage. "What do you have to do with this?"

His piercing blue eyes flicked over her, nothing like the soft blue of Cameron's. Her heart fluttered in fear, though she was still captivated.

"I cannot say much, but know that I am not a willing participant in this matter," he said, face solemn.

A small part of Nola's mind relaxed at the admission. *Sounds a lot like my life.* "And why are you telling me this?" she asked.

He gestured with one arm to the silvery puddle. "You were about to walk into it."

Inwardly, Nola cringed at the stupid question. "So what is

it?"

"I cannot tell you."

Frustration built up in Nola, but as she was about to open her mouth, he continued, "But it is a shame." The guilt on his face looked genuine.

"Can you tell me why?" Nola prodded.

Briar gave her an evaluating look. "We should speak elsewhere, human girl."

"Nola," she shot back at him. Her heart pounded. *I shouldn't be speaking with this faerie. Especially not wherever* elsewhere *is. But I need to do this. I finally have a lead.*

His smile could probably charm anyone and certainly caused a fluttery feeling in Nola's stomach as he said, "Nola."

She had the sudden urge to walk toward him and also run away and hide. Luckily, her feet obeyed her and she did neither. "Good," she forced out. *I'll have to ask Nameless if faeries have any sort of seductive powers. Maybe I gave him my name too freely,* she worried as she tried to look outwardly confident.

Not waiting for her to respond, Briar led her to their right until they were at the edge of what Nola called the wetlands. Her sneakers squelched in the mud as they walked through the calf-length grasses, but she paid it no mind. Briar didn't seem to mind either, placing his bare feet through it with grace. Nola studied his wings with eager eyes. Though they were folded, she tried to memorize every detail she could see of the intricate blue-black sections of membrane that were outlined in pure black.

She broke out of her thoughts as he stopped and turned, only a few inches from her now. Nola stepped back, only then noticing the thickness in the air around them.

"What are you doing with the water?" she asked him,

surprising herself by actually making eye contact as she did so.

Briar's eyebrows lifted in pleasant surprise. "I've made a barrier around us so that others cannot hear our words."

Interesting. She wanted to ask more, but feared he would fly away before she got any real answers.

"What else can you do?"

Briar gave her a short laugh. "Now, I can't give away all of my secrets right from the start now can I?" His look remained amused as he said, "I would have thought a certain someone would have told you all that by now."

"She has not had much reason to trust me so far," Nola jumped to the defense of the other faerie.

To her surprise, Briar nodded. Then he spread his arms wide. "What do you wish to know, Nola?"

She had a question ready. "Who are the faeries controlling the cloaks?"

He let out a startled laugh. "I truly wish I could tell you, Nola." He said her name again in that slow way, as if pleased with the way it sounded.

No. Don't get distracted.

"What can you tell me?" she asked. "What's in it for you? What's the magic for?"

He cocked his head to the side. "Many, many reasons."

Frustration building, Nola frantically tried to think of a more direct question, a more defined one.

She narrowed her eyes as it came to her. "You have not told me to keep the source of the gray stuff from the purple faerie."

"Perhaps it is time she knew." He stared at the nails of one hand.

"Then why don't you tell her yourself?" Nola gave him an

incredulous look.

"Those I work for would not appreciate that."

He really isn't into this whole enemy thing despite all he's done.

Nola took a chance and asked the big question. "Why were you banished here?"

"Would you believe it was forced upon me?"

"Maybe," she said slowly.

Briar was silent for a few seconds. Then he spoke softly, a vulnerable look coming into his eyes. "There is so much you do not know. It is better that way. Too many dangers go unseen and unchecked."

Nola stared at him, at a loss for words.

"Would it ease your mind to know that you could stop it?" he asked, a lightness coming back into his voice.

"How would I do that?" she asked skeptically.

"I do not know. You have the potential, though."

Nola resisted the urge to roll her eyes at the non-answer. But he was answering her questions. He was being nice to her. *What kind of enemy did that?*

He stepped forward then. "If you keep our conversations between us, perhaps I can tell you more."

She merely stared at him, mouth slightly open. In one quick motion, he pressed his lips to her cheek. Then, in true faerie fashion, he spread his wings and took off straight into the air, the blue in his dark wings glinting in the sun.

Nola stared up at his retreating form, cheek tingling where his lips had been and fingers itching to draw him again as he last looked at her. The vulnerability made him look softer, more human.

Sighing and shaking her head, Nola started to retrace her steps home. She didn't like the feeling of being played with, but there was something about Briar that endeared him to her. *I wish I could put my finger on what.* This felt familiar to what she had felt for Cameron not too long ago, that knowledge setting her whole body on edge. But it was also a welcome feeling.

Nola shook her head, forcefully. *He is a faerie and I am human. Plus he is sketchy. I will not fantasize about him.*

She turned her thoughts to practical matters. *I'll let Nameless know about the source tomorrow.* Guilt spread through her at the secret she was still keeping, though.

I just hope Nameless will forgive me when the time comes. And that Briar will not try to destroy me.

Chapter 23

Kelty stood outside her home tree, arms crossed, storm of emotions visible on her face. The leaves of her tree rustled as they picked up on her energy. It was Saturday, and so the trees alerted her to Nola's presence in the wood earlier in the day than usual.

Nola stepped into the clearing with a tentative smile on her face. That smile then slipped as she saw Kelty's expression, but the brave girl took a deep breath and took another step forward.

"I found the source," she said.

Kelty's eyebrows shot up, momentarily brought out of her mood. She straightened from her leaning position. "How?"

Nola took a deep breath. "I followed Briar to it."

Kelty gave her a hard look. "That was dangerous. I told you to stay away from him."

"And then we would be nowhere," Nola shot back at her.

The girl has a point. But I will speak to her of this later. She does not know the true danger.

"Take me," Kelty ordered sourly.

Nola led the faerie to a spot among thick vegetation, some-where closer to her dwelling than to the park. Something felt off about this spot, making Kelty squirm even though she was far from it. Nola brushed aside some leafy branches, and then she saw it, a brightness on the ground that shone a little bit more than that of the trees and roots.

Kelty froze, eyes wide, every inch of her going cold.

Briar. How could he? Kelty thought in anger and disgust.

Kelty approached the silvery puddle slowly with great reverence. She swept her arm to the side, coaxing the bushes to move to reveal all of it.

"What is it?" Nola asked quietly.

Kelty didn't look up. "The remains of a faerie."

Nola gagged. "I ingested dead faerie?" The girl put both hands over her stomach and started pacing. "What, do you just melt when you die?"

Kelty winced and threw her an annoyed look. "Over time, yes, if not properly returned to the *ara* by one powerful enough."

A visible shiver went through Nola's body. She took a breath and stopped pacing. "Well, are you powerful enough to, uh—"

"Yes," Kelty answered. "However, it may be that the faerie cannot be returned to the *ara* in this world, given that it is so weak."

Nola's face fell a little. "All you can do is try, right?"

"Yes," Kelty agreed, still looking disturbed.

"Does that make me part faerie now?" Nola asked quietly, cocking her head to the side.

"I do not know," Kelty said tersely. "I need to concentrate."

The girl fell silent. Then with a whispered, "I'm sorry," she turned and fled back into the wood.

Kelty heaved a sigh. *I will speak with her later. This cannot wait.*

She studied the fallen faerie closer. It was considerably smaller than other remains she had seen in her nineteen years of life. *Humans took some of it,* Kelty reminded herself. The size of the puddle shook her none the less.

Kneeling in the soil next to it, Kelty took a breath in and touched both of her hands lightly to the substance. A flood of feelings overwhelmed her: confusion, desperation, loneliness, but mostly fear. This faerie had been afraid at the time of death.

Tears flowed down Kelty's face as she forced her hands to keep steady. *Only emotions*, she reminded herself. There was no telling the circumstances of this faerie's death. And most were afraid of the unknown that lay beyond physical life.

Gathering her power, Kelty sent it slowly into the silvery puddle. *Rest easy, faerie.* Under her gentle hands, the energy within the substance calmed. It gradually began to seep into the soil under Kelty's guidance.

It wasn't long before she felt her power draining, straining to finish the job. Yet, she forged on, tears dropping from her cheeks to mix with the silvery substance.

No being deserves to die alone and remain forever trapped above the ground.

Her body trembled, fighting to send the last of the faerie's essence down into the ground when she felt a warm hand on her arm, and a burst of energy flowed to join with hers.

A flash of memory, the violation of Briar's magic touching hers in Faerie, made her want to jerk back. But the importance of her task kept her strong. And this magic was warm and comforting, nothing like the startling coolness of Briar's.

When the last of it had gone and was absorbed by the *ara* in the earth, Kelty let go of the soul energy with one final goodbye. She sat slowly, wiping tears from her eyes.

One green arm came into view, hand extended. She stared at it, a knowing stirring in the back of her mind. Kelty looked up at the watcher as the truth hit her.

Eyes wide, she stared at the glowing ball at his core, energy that called to her, igniting something warm within her. Only potentials were able to combine magic.

The watcher retracted his hand, letting it drop to his side. He looked a little nervous, but not as shocked as she.

It was only a sign of what could be. When souls were brought together that had the potential to connect on a deeper level as partners, their souls shone for one another. Whether or not that turned into a lifelong partnership was up to the pair, their souls bound once they both made a conscious choice.

Why the watcher? And why now? Her thoughts whirled as she tried to puzzle it out through the shock.

His voice broke into her thoughts. "My name is Rowan."

Kelty blinked at him. All she could do was nod.

I can't do this now. "The faerie felt fear," she said abruptly, breaking away from his gaze and gesturing to where the faerie remains had once been.

Rowan furrowed his brow. "Did you see any visions?"

Kelty shook her head. Those with the gift of spirit were known to be able to read visions of the faerie essence, if clear enough. "I have never been able to, just the feelings."

"Then we do not know definitively what occurred or where." Rowan said it as if he meant a comfort, but it only reminded Kelty that they did not know much about the happenings of this world, even the ones that involved their own kind.

"You used spirit," he went on unnecessarily.

"Yes." Kelty stood. "If anyone saw, let them come for me. This needs to stop."

She thought she saw a spark of agreement in his eyes.

"We need to find out who did this, faerie or human," Kelty said. She studied her new potential partner, wanting to ask if he would do more than watch this time, but at the last second keeping the question to herself.

Rowan nodded. "Yes, Star."

Chapter 24

Nola ran through the wood, one hand pressed to her stomach, not caring if anyone saw. *I swallowed dead faerie.*

And worse, Briar had pretty much been admitting to murder as they talked last night. *Well, maybe not murder, but something close to it. That poor dead faerie.*

She ran without direction, only slowing once to catch her breath. As she panted, she glanced around to gauge her whereabouts. A flash of blue amongst the leaves above had her running back in the direction she had come. *No, no, no. I can't see him right now.*

Eventually, Nola's lungs would not allow her to run anymore. She slowed to a walk, glancing above for signs of Briar. Her shoulders relaxed as she beheld only the familiar sights and sounds of the wood. Looking ahead, she recognized the path she was on as the one that led to the lily pond. *Good. Anything to distract me right now.* She kept going. *I wonder if the roots are still growing in the cabin.*

A thrill went through Nola as she arrived at the stone structure. It looked the same from the outside, but the roots and vines covered the walls of the inside as if reinforcing them. The sight gave Nola hope.

I feel bad for the faerie that died, but given the chance, I wouldn't give my power or my sight up for anything. As annoying as these faeries are, I would rather spend time with them than humans.

Nola's eyes widened at her own thought. *Is that because of the substance within me? Or would I have felt the same being boring old Nola?* She didn't have an answer for that one. She only hoped her sight wouldn't fade over time.

She ran a hand over the roots and vines, the life energy within them calming her. *I wonder if Derek knows what the gray stuff is,* she thought. Maybe the benefactors told him. Somehow, she doubted the others knew, though.

Nola approached the fireplace, the only surface of the cabin not covered by plant life.

Figures. I wouldn't want to be near this stuff for long either. Then it hit her. The vials. *Are they still here?* Nola reached into the opening and removed the forgotten box that contained the vials from behind the stone. Her hand tingled unpleasantly.

These need to go. Stuffing the box into her pack, Nola quickly made her way out the door and closed it behind her. Turning to continue back the way she came, she almost ran right into a tall figure in a black cloak.

Jumping violently back, Nola put a hand to her heart. "Derek!"

"What are you doing?" he said, a touch of annoyance in his voice.

"I—uh," Nola searched her mind frantically. "I wanted to see what the roots had done to the cabin."

Please believe me, she thought, shouldering her pack a little more behind her back.

He didn't even react to that. "Step aside." He went to move past her.

Nola stepped away and watched with growing dread as he

133

opened the door to the cabin. "It's not very usable anymore. The roots and vines are covering everything—"

"Yes." Derek cut in, pulling a flask out of his cloak. "There is a bad energy here."

He tossed the contents of the flask onto the plant life.

"What are you doing?" Nola asked, twisting her hands together.

"We have no need of this place anymore," he said simply.

Nola lunged forward in horror, but he had already flicked a match to life and tossed it onto the liquid. A flame immediately erupted from the space, bringing with it the noxious scent of gasoline.

Derek passed her on his way out. "Don't try to put it out. You will only hurt yourself. And don't go in for the vials. We have plenty more."

Unable to say anything, Nola merely stared at the increasing flames as he left. *No, no, no,* her mind screamed. She felt a tight sensation coming from the cabin, as if the energy was being sucked out of it. She saw the glow of the roots fading as they turned to black. It was making it hard for her to breathe. She looked around frantically for something to use to put the fire out. It was daylight, so someone would see it eventually and call the fire department, but that would likely be too late.

The pond. But I don't have a bucket or anything. She looked above, wishing she had a way to contact Nameless.

"What a pitiful sight."

Briar touched down next to her, looking disgusted, but not terribly worried about the fire.

"Can you put it out?" Nola asked him desperately, pushing aside for the moment whatever feelings she had.

He covered his nose from the smoke. "Yes."

Nola gave him an incredulous look when he moved no further. "So do it."

Briar raised an eyebrow at her. "What will I get in return?"

"You're a faerie. Aren't you supposed to put nature first?" Nola coughed as she finished the question.

"In Faerie, yes."

Freaking jerk. "What do you want?"

He studied her for a moment, causing Nola's nerves to skyrocket as she glanced back at the flames. *We don't have time for this.*

"I want you to listen to a proposition at a later time."

"What?" Nola stared at him, then shook her head. *Where are you, Nameless?* "Whatever, sure," she said.

Briar gave her that seductive smile and then looked toward the water. The energy at his core became almost blinding to Nola's sight. The surface began to ripple and pulse into a wave. The water then surged up onto the shore and continued into the cabin, seeping in through the cracks in the walls. It gradually quieted the flames until all that was left was blackened remains within the skeleton of a structure. It then retreated back to the pond, becoming calm once more.

With effort, Nola shut her mouth. She turned back to Briar. The smirk was gone from his face, a look of peace replacing it. Looking at the beautiful faerie, she found it difficult to imagine him as the enemy.

Then Briar frowned and looked up at the sky. "I must go," he told her, taking off in a small gust of air.

Nola stared after him, not at all sure what to think about what just happened.

Chapter 25

Kelty's head snapped up as a sharp current of energy shot up through her feet. Sending a bit of her magic into the trees to reveal a path, she took off in the direction of the disturbance in the *ara*, leaving Rowan to choose whether or not to follow.

The pond came into view in the distance as well as a plume of smoke coming from about where the cabin was. *Filthy humans,* Kelty fumed as she landed among the tree canopy. She could hear their voices now, shouting out for water and to call the fire department.

The *ara* within her twisted and whirled as the life she personally had fostered in the cabin slowly disappeared. She clenched her teeth, wanting to investigate, but knowing the area would be crawling with humans.

Kelty sensed him then, a slight thickening in the moisture of the air and a scent that promised rain. Briar. She just knew he was behind the dead faerie. Kelty gathered what little magic she had left. He would explain himself this time.

In a daring move, she dove straight through the leaves to grab the blue one, catching him by surprise. Kelty gripped his arm and gave him a harsh spin midair so that he faltered and almost crashed to the ground. She landed lightly on her feet and pushed the blue faerie over onto his back, one knee on his chest. Entirely thrown off guard, Briar looked back up at her apprehensively, though he still managed to quirk a quizzical eyebrow.

"How dare you defile one of our own like this," Kelty said in a voice of dangerous quiet.

His eyes went a little wide at that. "You do not know what was at stake."

"Pathetic excuse," she nearly spat at him. "Why? Why did you kill that faerie?"

Roots sprung from the ground around Briar to pin him there. Kelty looked up in surprise at Rowan as he strolled up to them. She gave him a slight nod in appreciation. Her limbs shook a little as she stood, still weak from the energy it took to guide the dead faerie back to the *ara*.

Briar made no attempt to fight off the binds. He eyed the green faerie with interest. "Who is your friend?"

Rowan merely stared at him, arms crossed, as if he hadn't heard the question.

"You will tell me what you know." Kelty glared down at Briar.

"Nameless," a familiar voice drifted out of the trees. A second later, Nola crashed through the bushes to their left.

"He put out the fire," she panted. "Derek set fire to the cabin and Briar put it out."

"What?" Kelty ground out. Surprise washed away a little of Kelty's anger, but the feelings from the dead faerie were still fresh on her mind. "One good deed does not make up for countless bad ones."

"No, but maybe you shouldn't be attacking him until you know it was him that killed the faerie," Nola challenged her. Then she backtracked a little, a slight cringe on her face. "Do you know it was him?"

Kelty stared at her. *She is sticking up for him. I should've seen this coming.* Kelty turned furious eyes on Briar. "What have you been telling her?"

Briar coughed. "Nothing."

This just keeps getting better. "He is a liar, Nola." She turned back to the girl.

"Maybe, but he hasn't destroyed us yet, has he?" Nola retorted. "What if the others are the ones behind everything?"

"Anything to say to that, Briar?" Kelty asked, eyes still on Nola.

"You need me," was all he said.

Kelty closed her eyes in frustration. Briar still held all of the answers. Killing him would do no good. *If his earlier words were true, and he really did bring me here to stop this, we may even be on the same side.*

In this situation, maybe he was the enemy they wanted.

Wait and watch and do what you can until the time is right. Never, never strike unless you can win.

It wasn't time to strike, not yet. Kelty opened her eyes and pinned Briar with her gaze.

"I'll play your game," she told him, nodding at Rowan to release the roots. "But I will end you if you involve Nola any more than she is now."

"Nameless," Nola cried, an angry blush rising in her cheeks.

Briar nodded at Kelty, an earnest look on his face that elicited one of pure shock from her. Then he gave Nola a small smile before spreading his dark wings and flying off.

Chapter 26

Nola's eyes tracked Briar until he disappeared from sight.

Kelty spun around, silver eyes blazing. "You should be more careful, human girl."

Oh, we're back to human girl, are we? Nola's heart raced. "You know I am right."

Despite her brave words, Nola shook. *Why did I do that? Why did I just save the enemy?*

"That does not mean he will not kill you," Kelty said. "Briar is not in control of this group. There are others making the decisions." She paused. "And he is a master of lies and deceit. I was cast out of Faerie because he lured me into a trap and used magic and his position as my potential to make it look like we accepted the partnership, which is forbidden."

What? Nola tried to follow the story, but the words came out of Kelty in a rush, tears gathering in her eyes.

"He will not hesitate to take everything from you," Kelty finished.

Wow. So he really did screw up her life. But that doesn't mean it will be the same with me.

"I'm in danger no matter what, Nameless. I was from the moment Derek forced that...stuff down my throat." She couldn't bring herself to say the words *dead faerie*. "And what are potentials?"

Kelty sighed and ran a hand through her long hair. "Two faeries can be potentials until they accept the partnership for life," she said.

"You are explaining that more to me later." Nola turned to throw Rowan a curious look. "I see you have decided to join. Will you tell me your name now?"

He gave her an unappreciative look. "And you have been speaking with the enemy. Once you explain, you may call me Rowan."

"Briar found me the other night and hinted that he is involved with the cloaks," she admitted to them both.

Kelty got in her face again. "What else do you know?"

Nola spread her hands in an appeasing gesture and stepped back. "That is all as far as I can tell. He speaks in riddles and lies—well, half-truths."

Well, that was the truth.

Both faeries studied her, causing her to squirm. "And what have you two been up to?" she threw back at them.

They both looked down at that. Kelty shifted her feet. "It is complicated," she said with finality as she looked back up. Her eyes dared Nola to comment further.

This got so much more complicated than I imagined it would.

Nola sighed. "Were you able to...lay the dead faerie to rest?"

Kelty nodded solemnly. "Yes."

"You don't know who it was?"

"All that matters is that the faerie felt fear at death," Kelty said, eyes taking on a far-off sheen.

"How do you know that?"

Kelty gave her that look that said she did not want to answer, but she said vaguely, "I could sense it."

Right, don't tell the human girl everything, she sighed inwardly.

"Okay, I think we should all get on the same page," Nola said, glancing back and forth between them. "What do we do now? The source is gone, but that still leaves all of the magic my father has and all that the cloaks have." She ticked their problems off on her fingers. "And we still don't know who is actually behind this."

Kelty shook her head and began to pace. "We need to find out who killed the faerie and brought it here. They are the masterminds."

"And we need to destroy the magic the humans have created," Nola added.

Kelty cringed. "Briar took the vial of black death from me," she admitted.

Nola slipped off her pack. She removed the box she had taken from the cabin and handed it to Kelty, who took it with a bit of a sour face.

"Here's some more to practice on. Do you think you will eventually be able to destroy it?" Nola asked her.

"Yes," Kelty answered. A determination shone in her eyes as she glared at the wooden box in her hands.

"Good. Well, right now what we can actually do is remove the magic and figure out how to destroy it, right?" Nola said. "The big meeting for their reward or whatever is Monday night. Maybe I can get them to bring what magic they have left."

Kelty frowned at her. "That will not take care of the bigger problem."

"It will buy us some time," Nola shot back.

Kelty lifted an eyebrow at Rowan, surprising both the green faerie and Nola. His eyes darted back and forth between them. "The girl is right. By destroying the magic, we send a message to those in power."

"Fine," Kelty said. She looked at Nola. "You will switch out the vials in your home and secure the rest the humans have." Her gaze shifted to Rowan. "We will figure out how to destroy the dark magic. And we will all be at the meeting to sabotage the humans, and to apprehend Briar."

Though the last sentence concerned Nola as well, Kelty's eyes remained on Rowan. There was a question in her gaze as well as a little shyness. Rowan nodded back at her, a warm look in his eyes.

They are acting strange. Nola shifted from foot to foot, not wanting to break into the moment. *But we are finally getting somewhere.*

* * *

Nola tried to take comfort from the sun peeking over the horizon Monday morning, her stomach churning in anticipation.

Today was the day. Phase one: school.

She ate breakfast quickly and waved goodbye to her parents as she rushed out the door to school. Today she paused a little to regard her father, who was staring absently into his bowl of oatmeal. For the first time since this whole thing started, her heart went out to him. *I hope he doesn't lose his job over this. Or worse.*

She planned to take the vials from the basement tonight after school, using the key she stole from her father's lab coat. The demonstration would happen tonight, whatever that meant. I still have to get them to bring whatever vials they have left tonight and get through the day without them suspecting me.

Nola got to school in record time, nerves giving her unusual speed. Jeanine met her at the top of the steps like she had ever since Nola joined the cloaks. They walked to class in silence.

The morning classes went by slowly as Nola kept glancing at the clock. Finally, lunch rolled around and she made her way to the table the cloaks made her sit at. The temptation was great to check out what Lauren and Tris were doing at their old table, but Nola looked straight past them. *It will do no good to worry about them today.*

She sat down across from Derek, who barely spared her a glance before he looked down again. Jeanine and Adam appeared like their normal selves, but next to her, Cameron jiggled his leg a bit. *I wonder if he is still having second thoughts.*

"The cabin is still standing." Derek's voice broke into Nola's thoughts. She realized he was looking at her.

"Yeah," she scrambled. "Luckily someone nearby had a bucket. With help we were able to put it out using the pond water." She schooled her facial expression smooth. *That sounded like the lie it was.*

"What of the vials in the fireplace?" Adam asked.

No, no, no. "I grabbed them before the firefighters could find them," she said quickly. "I can bring them tonight if you want."

Derek studied her a moment before nodding. Nola tried not to sag in relief.

"We are meeting at the gazebo, right?" Jeanine asked.

A hint of irritation showed in Derek's expression. "Yes."

"This is a new substance you made?" Nola asked.

"This one will be awesome," Adam answered her from across the table.

"Will you be testing the other ones, too? Or just this new

143

one?" Nola asked before Derek could say anything.

"No," Derek said shortly. *He never gives anything away. And I can't look too interested all of a sudden.*

The bell rang, startling Nola. *No, no, no,* she thought as everyone stood. *I need more time to figure out where the other vials are.*

Derek, Jeanine, and Adam strode forward out of the cafeteria, while Cameron hung back. He had been uncharacteristically silent during lunch.

Taking a chance, Nola grabbed his arm. "Do you want out of this?" she whispered.

He looked at her and nodded, eyes widening slightly.

"Get them to bring all of the vials with them tonight," was all she had time to say before Jeanine glanced back at them and frowned.

Nola made a show of taking Cameron's arm as if she was flirting with him, and after a moment the older girl turned back dismissively.

Cameron remained silent as they walked off to class.

Please, please actually do this tonight, Nola thought at him.

Chapter 27

Kelty sat, legs crossed, on the ground in front of her home tree. The growing darkness of the coming night was soothing as it settled over her, though the quiet that was left behind was unsettling. The animals withdrew from the area, and the leaves stilled as if the air itself was afraid to stir.

She held the vial of black Nola stole from the cabin out in front of her face. It swirled lazily, giving off that eerie dark energy. *You will not beat me.*

"It feels like death," Rowan's awed voice drifted to Kelty from where he stood among the trees a few paces behind her.

Kelty didn't take her eyes off the substance. "That is what we call it. You have not seen it before?" she called back curiously. It wasn't clear how long he had been in the wood, as good as he was at disguising his movements.

"I was sent to watch *you*," was his reply.

Gathering her magic, Kelty dug the sides of her feet into the soil. Through her legs and the tips of her wings, she absorbed the *ara* of the land, only probing the dark substance after drawing enough life energy into her that she tingled with warmth.

Kelty's breath froze in her chest as the extra energy was immediately drained, ripped from her. Wincing, she pulled back, withdrawing the rest of her magic into her core. Her breath started up again and she forced her shaking hands to still around the vial, though she longed to throw the substance far, far away.

A warm hand landed on her shoulder, sending a current of energy down her arm to settle in her core. Her body relaxed.

"You cannot break it," Rowan said matter-of-factly.

Kelty's brows pulled together as she looked over her shoulder at him. Shame twisted in her gut. *A human substance has bested the Star.*

"It drains life instantly." She searched his face for any indication he felt the same disappointment in her that she felt in herself.

Rowan's steady gaze revealed nothing but kindness and curiosity. "You will find the answer," he said with confidence.

Kelty sighed. "What makes you so sure?"

His hand slipped from her shoulder and the corner of his lips quirked up. "Stars shine brightest in the dark." Rowan held her gaze as he stepped backwards, giving her room to try again.

For a moment, Kelty forgot the vial of death in her hands as she repeated the words in her head. She never wanted to forget them or the warmth that spread through her body at the look in his eyes.

Rowan's gaze dropped from hers to her hands. Kelty blinked and brought herself back to the situation at hand. *You do not have time for this. And you still barely know anything about him.* She focused again on the swirling black.

"Human hands making human substances," she muttered as she recalled Nola's words. "The humans need to make it. It may be beyond the power of a faerie. Humans do not have magic, but they have iron and science. Maybe that is what is needed to dispel it." She paused as it hit her. "Or maybe the *ara* of the human world will be enough."

Rowan said nothing, but she forged on anyway, driven by a need for answers, a need to prove herself. This very action was what she had feared before, that the *ara* would be consumed like when Derek set it upon the wood. But with her guidance, the energy of the human world just might be enough to snuff out the darkness.

Holding her breath, Kelty scooped out a hole in the soil with her hand. Placing the vial inside, she covered it back up and placed both hands over the small mound.

Life, life to chase out the death.

Kelty sent her magic beneath the ground, calling to the trees through their roots. They answered, growing and twisting around the vial, their magic a hum vibrating up through the soil. She coaxed until the power grew to the point the land heated beneath her palms.

She took a deep breath, and on her exhale, she guided the energy to surround the substance. The *ara* encased the vial in light that shone from the cracks in the mound of soil. Then Kelty directed the magic surrounding the black death inward in one quick burst. A wave of energy rocked through the soil in the clearing before dissipating.

Kelty sent her magic through her hands and feet to soothe and repair the damage. A smile split her face when she found no trace of the black death left behind.

Eagerly, she turned back to find Rowan. "It worked—"

The smile slipped from her face as she stared at the empty space where her potential had stood. *He left.* Tears pricked at her eyes as her body went numb. *Why?*

She sent her power down, searching with the help of the trees.

She found nothing except a small burst of energy a few paces away. With a frown, she rose on shaky legs and stumbled over to a place not far from where Rowan had been.

The Telk stone that had been around his neck lay abandoned on the ground.

Chapter 28

He is in my room. There is a faerie in my room.

Nola stared at Briar. He gave her a casual look from his reclined position on her bed, at odds with her ordinary wooden nightstand, wardrobe, and desk. The darkness of him stood out painfully against her sky blue bedspread.

"What are you *doing* here?" Nola whispered as she shut the door, heart starting to race.

Briar remained where he was, head propped up on one hand, arm on her pillow. "Today is the big reveal." He gave her a smile. "I thought I would check in on the movements of my favorite human faerie. Make sure she stays out of trouble."

Human faerie. Is that how he sees me? Nola wasn't sure how to feel about that. Then she mentally shook herself. "You are here to sabotage me," she said with a frown, crossing her arms and leaning back against her dresser.

"That is one way to look at it." He sat up then, regarding her curiously. His black wings were spread on either side of him, somehow making him look more innocent despite the sharpness to his gaze.

Nola's mind spun. *How do I get out of this? Think, Nola. He is the enemy, but he also will probably let you out of this somehow.* She thought of Briar's willingness to talk to her after she found the source. *Think.*

"At the cabin, you said you had a proposition for me," she said the first thing that came to mind to distract him. "What was it?"

Briar let out a breathy laugh. "Oh, it is not time for that, Nola."

The way he said her name made her legs weak. She forced herself to focus on his words. "Why not? What is that supposed to mean?"

"Nola," her mother's voice came from below. Nola slapped a hand over her mouth. *Crap. They heard.*

"Yes?" she called back. Briar smirked at her from the bed and she gave him a dirty look.

"We're leaving. We'll be at game night until late. Dinner is in the fridge."

Nola nearly collapsed in relief. "Okay," she answered.

"They couldn't see me," Briar said matter-of-factly.

"How did you get in here?" Nola rounded on him as the sound of the car starting came from the driveway at the front of the house. "You better not have done anything to them."

He sighed, as if put out she would believe him capable of such a thing. "I merely snuck in behind them. They cannot see what is hidden by magic."

"How do you do it?" Nola couldn't help but ask the question.

"There is water all around us. I arrange it to disguise myself." He said it like they were discussing the weather.

Right. Her heartbeat sped a little more then. *I have to start remembering what he is capable of. I'm made mostly of water.*

Nola glanced toward the door. *How do I get him out of here?* And then a daring idea came to her.

"Well, I don't have a lot of time," she looked him in the eye.

He still wants me around to listen to this proposition or whatever it is. And he looked guilty about the source. Maybe he will let me just do what I'm going to do.

"I suppose you will follow me no matter what I do?" she asked.

"Yes."

Nola took a breath. "I'm going to switch out the vials from the basement with fakes. You can just get more anyway, can't you?"

She waited, breath caught in her throat. *I hope this isn't a mistake.*

Briar rose from the bed, somehow making it look graceful despite the wings. "It's true. But what will you do with them?"

"Return them to where they belong." She gave him a hard look as he stood across from her.

Briar studied her another moment, then nodded. "It is what's right."

"Tell me you're not lying."

He gave a short laugh at that and his eyes gained a warmth as he said, "I am not lying, Nola. I will let you switch out the vials and do as you wish with them."

There was only one thing to do now. Nola let out a nervous breath. She opened her bedroom door, grabbed the small cloth bag out from behind her dresser and walked to the stairs, leaving him to follow. He did so on foot all the way to the basement stairs.

Nola was on edge by the time they got there. *He's still going to try to stop me at some point. He has to. But he won't attack me at least. Not if he wants me to listen to this proposition.* Her stomach still churned as she fumbled in her pocket for her father's key that she had copied a few days earlier. Then she made her way across the basement to the light switch.

Once the light flickered on, Briar's attention was caught by a pile of dead plants in the corner, eyes wide.

Nola winced. *Why can't Dad clean those up?*

"Sorry," she mumbled as she went to work twisting the combination lock to the code she memorized when she first broke in and stole the gray substance. "I should've warned you about that."

Briar blinked, recovering quickly, and peered over at her. "What are you doing?"

Cabinet now open, Nola quickly loaded the vials into a separate cloth bag she had brought with her. "Replacing the substance with something else," she said vaguely. "With any luck, Dad will just think the stuff spoiled."

He surprised her by stepping forward and holding his hand out. "Let me."

Nola looked up at him with narrow, suspicious eyes.

"I will let you have it back once you are done."

"I will do it," she said, shoving the final vials in and pulling the bag closed tight. Then she awkwardly grabbed the one filled with the counterfeits from the floor while still holding the bag with the vials of the real substance. *Not that he isn't capable of taking them from me after this,* she thought. *I have to convince him it really isn't a big part of the plan, it's something he can let slide.*

"This is my father's mess," she said. "I have to clean it up."

"This is not your father's doing."

"He found it and that's how Derek found it," Nola argued, placing the counterfeit vials carefully in the places she had removed the others from.

"And I suppose you think the human youths just stumbled

across a way to make this strange magic from it?" Briar said, eyebrows raised at her.

Nola paused. "All of it was planned?" She turned to Briar. "Was I planned?"

Briar shook his head. "No. That was the human's doing." His expression took on a softer look again.

Relaxing slightly, Nola finished and shut the cabinet. She clicked the lock shut and turned to face him.

"I'm assuming we will get to meet these criminal master-minds at some point?" she asked apprehensively.

Briar inclined his head silently.

Okay. Well, I don't have time now to poke him about that. "What now then?" she asked. "Are you going to let me leave?"

He cocked his head to the side. "What is it you plan to do?"

"I think you can figure it out."

A startled smile spread across his features. "You are a smart one." Then he sobered. "One day we will overcome this mess the both of us are trapped in, human faerie."

Briar bowed to her from the waist this time and with a dashing smile he turned and almost skipped up to the main floor and out of sight.

Nola stared after him, stunned. *That was interesting. Maybe he likes me more than I thought.* Her cheeks burned at the thought. *Or he just realized he should really be apprehending the cloaks and not me.*

With a sigh, she switched off the light and hurried to lock the basement door. *I need to get to the woods. They'll get suspicious if I'm not there.* Her stomach lurched as she thought about the night ahead.

Nola made it to the main floor and turned toward the front room. She only made it a few steps when she felt a resistance in the air in front of her, like she was moving through molasses.

A voice came from behind her. "I am sorry, but I cannot let you go that easy."

Slowly and with much effort, Nola turned to face Briar. *No, no, no. What are you doing?*

His expression was the opposite of mocking, guilt shining in his eyes. *He doesn't want to. But he is still going to do whatever it is.*

Nola tried to speak, but only succeeded in opening her lips slightly. Briar reached out and took her arms. She tried to struggle as terror came alive within her. *I can't move!*

He guided her to a seated position on the floor, her body obeying him despite the panic in her mind, and touched a finger to her forehead.

A coolness spread through her body at his touch. Nola tried to open her mouth again, her jaw refusing to cooperate entirely now. Her limbs felt like lead, the only parts of her seeming to function were her frantically beating heart and her lungs. She knew the panic shone in her eyes as she looked up at him. She didn't care. *Don't do this!*

"It will wear off gradually, but not for some time," Briar said. He gave her a look that was not unkind before straightening. As he turned to leave, his foot caught on the strings of the bag containing the vials, pushing it up against her leg. Then he disappeared around the corner of the hall, leaving Nola to her panicked thoughts.

Chapter 29

The cloaked humans entered the wood shortly after dusk. High above them, Kelty eyed their slow procession as she fingered the Telk stone that was now at her throat, the stone with the ability to take her back to Faerie.

I could go home. The thought had crossed her mind for the briefest of seconds as she picked it up from the ground, the magic within it almost pulsing, calling to her. But the temptation left her the next instant as her thoughts turned to Rowan. His disappearance was too sudden. And the fact that she held the Telk stone meant he was still in the human world.

Something is not right. Someone took him. Either the outcasts or the humans or both. Her magic churned within her core.

I will get him back.

Below, one of the cloaked figures pulled a wagon with a large boxy object covered by a cloth. The three others surrounded the wagon as they trudged down the stone path in the dim light. Kelty peered down at the box, then dropped silently to the ground behind a sturdy tree trunk as they passed by. This close to it, the tang of iron coming from underneath the cloth burned to her senses. She bared her teeth at it, pressing herself into the bark beside her.

It was then she noticed the absence of Nola's short-skirted

cloak. *They better not have done anything to her either.*

A rustle in the bushes drew her attention to the taller cloak on one side of the wagon. A few paces away, he straightened out of a stumble, continuing on after telling the others he was fine. He left behind a dark shape half concealed by the thin branches of a berry bush. Kelty dashed forward. The dark shape turned out to be a small, lumpy bag made of cloth.

It must contain the rest of the vials. Nola came through.

Kelty kept her sharp eyes on the cloaks as she reached for the bag.

In that moment, a strong scent of spring rain enveloped her. *Of course, it wouldn't be that easy.* Whirling around, she came face to face with Briar.

"Stay away," Kelty hissed, conscious of the fact that the humans were still nearby.

"You know I cannot do that," he said with a smirk, significantly louder than she had been.

Eyes wide, Kelty glanced sideways at the humans. They continued toward the gazebo. Her gaze snapped back to Briar.

"I need the vials," he said simply.

"You know I cannot do that," Kelty flung his words back at him.

Briar continued to look at her tauntingly, but he did not strike.

"Nola is not here to save you this time," Kelty said in a voice of quiet danger.

A laugh startled out of him that caused the humans to pause and look in their direction. Kelty froze, as Briar remained mercifully quiet for a moment. Seeming a little wary, Derek said, "Keep going."

There was no time for relief as Briar's first attack hit her. Water, gathered from the air around them, filled her mouth and nose, cutting off her airways. She continued to glare at Briar's smiling face, knowing panicking would only make it worse.

It would be easy to use her own power over water to counteract his, but that might prove dangerous still. It was likely the other outcasts were watching. This world knew of her use of spirit, but that was all. And Kelty wanted to keep it that way.

This is my wood and it will defend me.

Reaching downward with her power, Kelty allowed the roots of the tree to grow up and connect with her bare feet. *Absorb,* she ordered, feeling the water that clogged her mouth seeping through her body and out into the roots.

Wasting no time, she magically grabbed hold of the branches behind him, going for the wings. Briar dodged those, laughing as he did.

The sound irked Kelty. She didn't have time for this. And he knew it. He wasn't fighting that hard, just providing a distraction. *I need to end this quickly.*

Kelty struck again and again with the branches, starting to feel the effect of another standard water attack. Her mouth felt dry and her body slowed as she followed Briar, drying from the inside.

She took another shot at him, this time with a particularly long branch behind him. She missed, but his dodge had him leaping down towards her.

Kelty launched herself up at him at the same time. The surprise on his face was evident when she took hold of his arm midair, tugged them over to land on a wide branch and reached back to grab the edge of one of his wings with her other hand.

Briar's whole body froze at the very unfaerie-like move. "You fight dirty," he said tightly, not daring to move. A shredded wing meant no possible escape. Even his magical disappearances wouldn't work if he was injured.

"I learned from the humans," she said, face just inches from his. Her body itched to be away from Briar, his eyes still taunting her even in this position.

"What are we to do now?" he asked.

Thoughts of what the humans might be doing to the place she now thought of as home, the place that needed her, brought Kelty up short. *Home. When had it become home?*

Kelty blinked and focused once more on the choice she was to make. She could continue to fight Briar and risk losing the wood. She could shred his wings, an act of violence that would eat away at her conscience despite her animosity towards him. Or she could give him a reason not to interfere anymore.

"You will leave now and lay low for a while. You will tell your—" she searched for a word, "whoever has hold over you that I shredded your wings and you were forced to remain in hiding until they healed."

Kelty held her breath as she waited for his answer. She was counting on the fact that Briar really didn't want to be fighting them, that he truly brought her here in a disguised attempt to thwart the very faeries he was working for. *Please mean your words for once.*

He kept the smirk frozen on his face. "It will work," he finally said. "But you will have to do at least part of the job. They will be looking for evidence."

Kelty nodded. With a quick twist of her fingers, she tore the membrane at the edge of one wing so that streams of silver flowed down her fingers and dripped onto the tree. It would not hinder his flight entirely, allowing him to escape and hopefully convince the others of his story.

If he kept his word.

But Kelty didn't have time to worry about that. With one last hard look at Briar, which he answered with a smart nod despite the pain, she flew off to where she had last seen the humans.

Kelty dove down through the trees to get a glimpse of what was happening in the gazebo.

The cloaked humans had gathered like usual, though they seemed a little agitated in the open space. Two of them were arguing over something, arms flying in wild gestures. But Kelty's eyes looked past them to the head of the long table. On it sat a cage of wire and in it was Rowan, lying still.

Her breath caught in her throat. *Filthy humans!*

Frantically, Kelty probed with her power, searching for his. If they were partnered, she would feel when things like this happen. As it was, she could barely reach him through the cage of iron.

Kelty hissed and took off on foot through the trees toward him. Once close enough, she threw a quick glance at the humans. When she saw they were still arguing, she slipped out of the cover of the trees to assess the problem of the cage.

As she got closer, she could at least feel Rowan, though his essence was faint. His color was pale, too. *Iron poison.* Tears pricked at her eyes as she beheld her potential's still face.

She reached out with her power to the trees behind her, gathering their strength.

"Hey!"

"Another one!"

Kelty's concentration broke as something disturbed the humans. Dropping her hold on the plant life behind her, she turned to where they had been arguing.

The cloaks now stood staring directly at her.

159

Chapter 30

He locked me in my own house, my own body! A painful anger filled Nola. She tried to move. She screamed. The sound didn't leave her mouth.

They need me. Nameless has power, but she doesn't understand the humans like I do. Why am I always the one in these situations? Why do I let boys do this to me?

A tear slipped down her cheek. It started to itch, but she couldn't wipe it away. She gave another internal cry of frustration.

The feeling of betrayal was the worst. *He was the enemy, but he made me believe he wasn't. I wanted so badly to believe he wasn't.*

Eventually the anguish subsided a little to be replaced by fear of what would happen without her at the meeting. *Maybe this will wear off sooner than he planned,* she hoped. The bag of vials next to her leg caught her eye. *At least he didn't take them.*

Her breath caught in her chest. *He didn't take them.* He left her magic that might save her.

Nola focused all of her energy into trying to move her right arm. Her fingers twitched. *This is not happening. I will not sit here as my friends possibly die or my woods are destroyed, or both.*

She tried again. A little more movement, but still barely what she needed to reach the bag.

Another wave of frustration hit her. *If only I was a faerie.* Inspiration struck and she thought of the magic she now saw within the elements of the world. She pictured how it flowed out of Kelty to join with the magic of the plants. *Well, I have a tiny bit of that in me.*

Holding that thought in her mind, she tried to move again. Nothing more than a flicker.

Frustrated tears welled up as she closed her eyes, the only body part she could move besides the ones necessary to keep her alive. She went to that mental place again, for it was the only thing she could do. She pictured the soothing energy of the woods, the feeling of her feet in the grass, the comfort she felt when she ran from Derek and the cloaks. *I think the faeries have it right,* she thought. *Maybe some day I'll get to see what their world is like.*

A warmth spread through Nola, a calm. And then she willed the magic of the vials toward her.

She opened her eyes to find her hand closed over the bag, one of the vials under her pointer finger. *How did that happen? Did I do magic?*

Nola tried to grasp the vial, and surprisingly her hand obeyed this time, just very slowly. *I was thinking of the earth, of the life within it.* It hit her then. *Human faerie. I was thinking like a faerie.*

It took nearly ten minutes, but Nola was finally able to uncap the vial and raise it to her lips. As the substance slid down her throat, the muscles of her body started to slowly unlock as she became a little less human.

Chapter 31

The humans should not be able to see.

Kelty's magical shields were still intact. She remained frozen as they stared her down. Then Derek smiled crookedly and reached into his cloak.

She just had time to duck behind the cage before he threw the vial. It shattered against one of the wooden poles holding up the gazebo, dissolving it and part of the roof. A drop landed on the wooden table that Rowan's cage sat on, eating away at it. Heart in her throat, Kelty was about to leap toward him when the destruction halted.

Loathing filled her as she beheld her potential again, so still and devoid of life.

Humans destroy everything that is good!

Kelty gathered her magic, but Derek was faster. He leaped over the table with grace, reaching for her.

"Derek!"

The humans turned toward the other side of the gazebo, where Nola now stood panting, face alive with rage and purpose.

Nola! A small part of Kelty's mind relaxed to see the human girl alive and whole. Kelty's eyes narrowed as she realized the human had more of a glow to her. *What—no, no time for that now.*

Kelty took her chance to use the distraction. She threw her hands out as vines and branches from along the sides of the gazebo shot out to wrap around the cage. Kelty closed her fists and they ripped apart the metal. Rowan tumbled free to the ground. Kelty winced as he rolled and landed with one of his wings at an odd angle. *Not the best plan.*

A hand closed on her arm then and she spun furiously, lashing out with her power so that the ground trembled and branches whipped towards Derek. *Filthy human hands!*

Derek held on tight, eyes glinting as if this were a game. He slashed wildly at the branches with the knife that was now in his hand. Kelty ducked as the blade came dangerously close to cutting her.

"Derek! Whoever you are working for will be upset if you hurt her," Nola yelled as a distraction.

Derek paused just long enough for Kelty to command a branch to wrap around his neck. Violence in his eyes, he went for her with the knife. Kelty ducked and the tip of the knife gouged her arm. Hissing, she threw her power into other branches, securing Derek's knife arm and then his other arm and legs.

Her wound stung from the iron, its poison seeping slowly toward her core. *No, I will save us. We will not meet our end in this world of horror.* She forced the pain out of her mind.

Kelty locked eyes with Nola across the expanse of the wood structure. She was not comforted by the desperation she saw mirrored in the girl's eyes. *Get us out of this, human girl.*

"Do something!" Derek shouted.

Kelty whirled to head off one of the other boys now charging at her, but Nola yelled again, "Adam, stop or she will kill Derek."

Adam halted. Everyone froze.

Chapter 32

"Just hang on." Nola put up both hands in a calming gesture. "How can you guys see her?"

"Don't tell her," Derek said at the same time that Cameron said, "Eye drops."

The boys glared at one another, now apparently in open opposition.

A look into a world of magic. Nola recalled Cameron's words to her on the phone. *This will be harder now that they can see the faeries.*

Nola's mind worked frantically, the faerie essence now so much more present within her. She felt more alive and more confused than ever. *I have more power, but I have no clue how to use it. Especially against the humans. Awful as they are, I cannot hurt them. That's just not me.*

"I knew you were lying about something," Derek spat at Nola. The branch around his neck tightened as Kelty turned a furious glare on him. Nola eyed what she could see of Rowan now on the grass just beyond the gazebo. *How do we all get out of here alive?*

"Somebody stop her!" Derek yelled.

The others remained frozen, though Adam's expression of rage suggested he might just attack Kelty at any moment. She glared back at him daringly as branches wound around Derek's mouth, effectively muffling his outraged cries.

"She has more power than any of you," Nola said loudly. "I would let her be. And I don't know why you got into this mess, but I would walk away right now."

Jeanine sneered at Nola. "Our benefactors can take care of this...creature."

Kelty gave her a hiss, but it was a little halfhearted. Despite her bravado, Jeanine jumped and backed up a step, giving the faerie a wary look.

Ignoring her, Kelty went to kneel by Rowan.

"How do you know?" Nola asked. "Do you even know who these benefactors are?" She kept her eyes on Adam and Jeanine, though she remained aware of Cameron beside her.

The resounding silence spoke volumes.

"They communicate through notes," Cameron finally admitted.

"So you don't even know who they are, what they are?" Nola challenged.

Jeanine's eyes flashed at her. "They gave us this one." She threw her hand back in a casual gesture toward Rowan. "They are more powerful and they have promised us the same power." Her expression grew a little fanatic.

They did this to Rowan, this group of outcasts. They were going to make him into the next source. Nola worked to keep her face smooth as she came to this realization.

"Then why aren't they saving you now?" Nola crossed her arms.

All three exchanged fearful looks.

Nola sighed. "Get out of this now—all of you. Tell your benefactors—" Nola paused, searching her mind for exactly what would get them out of this with their lives.

"How do you know any of this?" Adam exploded, stalking back to Nola. Cameron made to step in front of her, one arm held out to ward off Adam's approach, but Nola squared her shoulders.

"I wouldn't come any farther if I were you," she said in a powerful voice. As he came forward just then, Nola had seen the flare of light in his eyes. Just his eyes. *I can feel it*, she realized.

Adam stopped and gave her an incredulous look. "Or you'll do what?"

Taking hold of the slight burst of power she felt behind his eyes, Nola magically prodded it. The magic came easily to her, combining with her own. Withdrawing back into herself with a snap, Nola stepped back slightly.

Adam furiously rubbed at his eyes. *Oh, no, please don't tell me I blinded him.*

"What's wrong with you?" Jeanine asked, tone almost accusatory.

"Nothing," Adam said defensively. He straightened up and opened his eyes. Nola noticed with relief that he still seemed to be able to see. *But he will not be able to see the faeries anymore.*

Adam went back to looking sinister. His looked slipped a little at the satisfied smile on her face. "What?"

Nola pointed behind him. "Look."

He did, slowly, keeping one eye on her. "I see nothing," he said, eyes widening after the words were out of his mouth. He backed up a step. Nola felt Cameron's evaluating eyes on her.

"Your benefactor didn't tell you about me, did he?" Nola couldn't help giving Derek, still gagged and bound, a look as she said this.

"How did you do that?" Adam yelled, an edge of hysteria creeping into his voice. "You are not one of them."

Nola gave him a look. "Am I not?" she said, raising an eyebrow. A thrill ran through her. *They are scared of me for once. They are scared of what they don't know.*

"You glow a little like them," Cameron said in an awed voice.

Just noticing that now, huh? Nola suppressed the urge to roll her eyes. She turned to the blond boy. "Do the eye drops or whatever wear off?"

He stared at her for a second. Then he blinked. "Uh, yeah, in a couple hours."

"Then you and Jeanine can keep your sight for now." Nola walked across the room with confidence, fixing Derek with a look. Out of the corner of her eye, she saw the flaring light coming from Kelty, flowing from the faerie's hands into Rowan, who was still pale and almost lifeless. Kelty's magic didn't look as strong as it should either. Nola cringed as she saw the wound on her arm seeping silver blood. *Oh, Nameless, hang on.*

Nola tuned out the others arguing behind her as she glared straight into Derek's eyes. "You do not deserve the sight," was all she said as she coaxed the magic from him. An outraged, muffled cry came from Derek and he struggled violently, the hand with the knife awkwardly slashing at his binds.

At that moment, Kelty cried out, a frustrated and agonizing sound. Nola automatically turned towards her.

"Nola!" she heard Cameron yell. And then a feeling of weightlessness took her as she was knocked backwards off her feet.

No, no, no. Nola watched as Derek slashed at the rest of his living binds and leapt at Kelty and Rowan.

167

Chapter 33

Live, Rowan.

Kelty gathered what magical strength she had that wasn't being sapped by keeping Derek captive or being taken by the iron poison seeping through her body and sent it into Rowan. She was never much of a healer, but she held out hope that their bond would do the rest of the work.

There was a tinge of iron to Rowan's magic, though not nearly enough as was seeping through her. Kelty winced at the state of his wings, torn and slick with silver, and what looked like burn marks, slashes on his chest. One large jagged wound in the middle of his chest seeped silver blood as well. *The iron cage when I broke it open,* Kelty thought with guilt.

The worst of it was that his essence, his soul, felt so far away. Try as she might, she could not reach him.

So little time. Tears fell from Kelty's eyes to fall onto Rowan's pale face. She thought of the *lumin* flower he brought her, the way he lent her the power to guide the dead faerie back to the *ara*, even the words that prompted her to get involved with the humans.

He gave me strength. Watching and believing and prodding me to become more than I was. So many things I never said.

Pressing her lips together in determination, Kelty drove her remaining power into his core, reaching out with one magical hand. *Live, Rowan. I want you to live.*

She spotted a tiny spark then. Straining forward with her magic, she grabbed hold of it, rejoicing at the connection. Eyes of warm brown flashed open and, connected as they were, she heard his voice in her mind. *If you wish me to, Star.*

Joy filled every inch of her being despite her weakened state and his. Almost every ounce of energy she had left flowed to him, giving him just enough strength to live, to survive.

She held his gaze as she removed his Telk stone from her throat and pressed it into his hands. *Go to Faerie,* she commanded. *Or I will be very angry with you.*

No words this time, but she felt his amusement.

And then she closed her eyes, arching her back at the sudden pain as her branches were slashed away. Wrenching herself free from Rowan, Kelty whirled around just in time to see Derek diving toward her.

Instinctively, Kelty rolled to the side so that Derek sailed past. There was a flash of light. And in the next moment both Rowan and Derek were gone, vanished into thin air.

There was a stunned silence as the humans stared, wide-eyed at the place where their leader and the green faerie had just been.

Kelty let out a startled laugh that caused the humans to all start yelling at once.

"Where is he?"

"Are you kidding?"

"You witch! Bring him back!"

"Guys. He's gone." Everyone quieted at Nola's words. Cameron helped her stand. She looked a little shaky, but otherwise unharmed. Nola turned to look at Kelty. "He's in

Faerie, isn't he?"

Kelty stared at the spot they had been and didn't answer. She gripped her arm and hoped Rowan would receive the help he needed, that what she had done had been enough for him to survive until he got real help from a healer of Faerie.

"Is he coming back?" Jeanine prodded, a note of hysteria making its way into her voice.

The faerie came back to herself as she realized the girl with the sneer was talking to her. "No," she answered.

There was another silence, charged with shock and fear. Nola was the one to break it.

"You guys should leave now and get yourselves out of this however you can—"

"Tell your benefactors that another protects you," Kelty cut Nola off in a weak voice. The girl stared at her in shock.

Adam sputtered at the faerie. "We don't need your protection—"

"Then die, human." Kelty pinned him with a sideways glare. Shocked into silence, he stared for a second and then turned and ran. After a second, Jeanine took off after him.

Pathetic humans.

Cameron turned to Nola. "You will be all right?"

Nola stared at him. "I'm fine."

Concern still etched onto his features, he stepped forward and pressed something into Nola's hand. With a quick nod at her and then a hesitant one at Kelty, he took off after the others.

Nola watched him go for a second, then tucked the object in her pocket as she rushed to Kelty's side. "That looks bad, Nameless," she said, eyes wide.

The faerie looked up at her. "My name is Kelty."

Chapter 34

You are not dying on me, Nola thought, not being able to think of another reason why the faerie would choose now to give up her name.

"How do faeries heal?" she asked, fingers nervously poised over Kelty's arm, unsure if she should touch her or not. "Is it magic? Can you heal yourself?"

Kelty winced. "No magic can cure the iron poison."

No, no, no. This is not happening. Not now. There has to be some way. Energy still pulsing through Nola, she focused on the faerie like she had the humans just a few minutes earlier. Kelty's essence was usually bright, but now reduced to a dim glow. A blackness was spreading slowly, coming from the wound on her arm.

Then a pair of startling silver eyes were very close to her own. "What did you do to yourself?" Kelty asked sharply.

What does that matter now, Nameless? "It's a long story. It can wait. Unless—" Nola suddenly glanced around. "Have you seen Briar?"

Kelty's eyes narrowed. "So he is responsible." The faerie took in a wheezing breath as she leaned back against the wooden pillar. "He will not be around for a while."

"I would like to hear that story," Nola said wryly. "But first we need to heal you."

"There are no healers here. And I cannot go back to Faerie," Kelty said dully.

"Guess I will just have to save you, then," Nola said with a confidence she didn't have. What she did have was a hope that with the added faerie essence within her, she could draw the poisonous iron out like she had the magic from Adam and Derek.

Kelty pinned Nola with her eyes again. "You do not know what the faerie magic will do to you."

"I feel good, Nameless."

"For now."

"What's done is done, right?" Nola gave her a perturbed look. "I don't care what happens to me. Now will you let me try to heal you or not?"

Kelty gave her a smile then with something like pride in it. "You sound like me," she said. "What a pair we are." Then she closed her eyes and seemed to sink into herself.

"Don't give up, Nameless."

The corner of Kelty's mouth quirked up, though her eyes remained closed. "Never."

That's the faerie I know.

Nola reached out with tentative fingers to touch Kelty's arm just below the wound. Her skin was startlingly smooth and a tad bit cold, though Nola wondered if the coldness came from her weakened state. *Focus,* she told herself. *You are a human faerie now. You can do this.*

This time, she dug into the human part of herself, the part that could handle iron. She imagined the tangy feel of the metal and called it to her like she had done with the magic behind Adam's eyes. The inky blackness did not respond.

172

So much for that. Stubborn human substance.

Her mind went back to just an hour or so prior when thinking of the energy in the world around them had led her to be able to clutch the bag.

Nola took a breath and thought of the woods once more. It was easier now that she was surrounded by the trees. She removed her shoes and socks, and the connection she felt with the nature around her instantly strengthened.

Feeling empowered, Nola tried to send her magic into Kelty's arm, focusing on the areas around the seeping blackness. Adding her strength to Kelty's, she coaxed the areas around it in an attempt to force the poison back. It resisted. *Out, stupid iron.* Nola threw all of her strength into it. Her body trembled and her breath came in short gasps, but she held on until the blackness was driven out of the faerie's body, oozing out of the wound. Nola felt a rush of pride as the wound also knitted together, skin smooth once more.

Nola snapped back to reality, a fatigue spreading through her. She looked down at her arms covered in both silver and black liquid and then at the pale, still faerie.

"Nameless," Nola muttered, reaching out to place a finger under her nose. She wasn't breathing.

Nola's heart seized. *Faeries breathe, I know that, but can they go without it? Should I do CPR?*

Then she shook her head. *I'm thinking like a human.* Opening herself up to the magic Nola still felt inside her, alive and bright despite contact with the iron in Kelty's wound, she focused on the faerie's core, shoulders sagging in relief once she found the faint light. *She's alive.*

But what did I do wrong? I got all the iron out.

A sudden rustle of leaves reminded Nola that they were still in the gazebo. *We can't stay here.*

Paranoia crept up her spine as she looked around. *We are way too exposed.* Nola put her shoes back on and gathered up Kelty awkwardly, though it was at least made easier by the fact that the faerie was slightly smaller. *She is going to hate me for this when she wakes up. If she wakes up.* Nola pushed that last thought from her mind as she tried not to crush Kelty's wings or drag them on the ground.

It took much longer than it should have to carry Kelty back to her tree. With shaking arms, Nola laid her on the dirt in front of the home she had never been invited into.

Nola rubbed her eyes and sat next to Kelty, at a loss for what to do. Tears fell from her eyes. *If she dies, it will be my fault. For stealing that vial. For getting her involved with the cloaks. For meddling in things I shouldn't have.*

Soft dawn light slowly chased away the darkness as Nola sat beside the faerie.

Please don't die on me, Nameless—Kelty.

Then there was a quiet rustle of leaves and a force that tugged at Nola's awareness. She reached into her pocket to clasp the knife as she stood. In one swift motion, she whirled in the direction of the magic, brandishing the knife awkwardly in front of her.

A handsome face of blue stared at Nola with wide eyes. Hate, pain, fondness, betrayal, all swirled within her as she stared at the faerie that had locked her in her own body. *But he also left you the way out,* an internal voice reminded her. *A way out that meant possibly changing you forever,* another voice argued. *He left you no choice.*

Wordlessly, they stared at each other. Nola noticed the blood covering one of his wings. The silver liquid was mesmerizing, containing so much life energy.

"What happened?" Briar asked, breaking the silence and snapping Nola back to reality. A look of genuine concern crossed his face, though his eyes remained wary.

I wonder what he sees in me now.

Nola kept the knife between them as she summarized, "Derek cut Nameless—uh, Kelty—with a knife. He then attacked her and Rowan. Somehow Derek ended up sucked into Faerie with Rowan." She risked a glance back at Kelty. "I thought I got all the iron poison out, but she has not woken up." Worry and fatigue suddenly made it hard to keep holding the knife.

"You did that?" Briar asked, awe in his voice.

"What did you think would happen when you left me no choice but to drink more of that stuff?" She still couldn't bring herself to say *dead faerie.*

He blinked. "It has changed you more than I expected," was all he said.

So you did plan on changing me, Nola thought. A harsh laugh escaped her. *That's all anyone ever does. Besides Kelty. Well, no more.*

Briar leaned back almost imperceptibly at her laugh and remained silent. *I call the shots now,* Nola realized. She savored the moment and then reminded herself of the situation.

Lowering the knife about a foot, Nola gestured back to Kelty. "Will she survive?"

He peered around her at the purple faerie. "The *ara* within her is very faint," he said quietly. "But the land will heal her."

What? Nola gave him a doubtful look. He gestured behind her.

She turned to see her faerie friend half wrapped in roots that were growing up from the soil. A light seeped from them,

175

flowing into Kelty. The arm holding the knife dropped to Nola's side at the sight. *Amazing.*

A moment later, she remembered the dangerous faerie that stood next to her. She brought up the knife again as she turned back to Briar. "Why did you come here?" Nola demanded, feeling that swirl of mixed emotions again as she looked at the one that adorned the pages of her notebook and played her like a fool.

Briar gave her an odd look as if he didn't know who she was anymore. His lips parted slightly, but then he shut them again. Then he said, "I do not know."

Nola nearly groaned in frustration. "Do faeries ever give straight answers?"

He made a sound like a laugh, but there was no humor in it. "Rarely."

Nola sighed. "Tell me what you want from me, Briar." Her fingers tightened on the knife and she shifted her feet.

Briar studied her, indecision in his eyes. Finally, he said, "I wanted to see that you were safe and well."

Nola's heart swelled despite the prior actions of the faerie in front of her. *This is so not fair.*

"Did you really?" She pointed the knife right at his face. "Truthfully?"

"Yes," he said.

"And what about now?" Nola forged on. "What happens now that Derek is gone? What happens to us?"

His eyes took on a haunted look. "Now the real battle begins. Someday, you will not hate me so much for what I've done."

What's that supposed to mean? Nola stared at him with wide eyes.

"Watch yourself, human faerie." He turned to go.

No, no, no. Nola was struck with a desperation at seeing him retreat. She hated herself for it, but she felt so exposed and alone, his words echoing in her head. *Now the real battle begins.*

"Wait!" she said. "You will tell me about this proposition eventually, right?"

He paused, glancing over his shoulder. A ghost of his trademark smirk crossed his face. "I have not forgotten, Nola."

Nola's heart skipped a beat as she let him go, watching him retreat into the trees on foot. *He will be back.* The thought was oddly comforting, despite knowing she should be disturbed. With a weary sigh, Nola collapsed on the ground next to Kelty, who was now, other than her face, covered in roots.

I wonder what she will think of all this.

Chapter 35

Kelty rested in a state of dark, blissful peace, the kind that came from having no worries, no more awareness other than of her soul in the darkness.

That peace slipped away little by little as a restlessness started to take over. A presence pulled her forward, a familiar one, one that brought up feelings of annoyance, but also fondness and pride.

You are not alone.

The midmorning sun blinded Kelty as she opened her eyes. Hissing, she immediately rolled over to her side, the roots that covered her retracting back into the ground.

"Nameless!" Nola jumped up. "I thought you might die!"

Kelty took a steadying breath, then gave her a look. "You've seen what happens when faeries die." Her voice came out quiet but strong.

"Yeah, but, well you could've been in a coma for all I knew—"

She raised an eyebrow at Nola. "A coma?"

"Nevermind," Nola waved an impatient hand. "How do you feel?"

"Alive." Kelty winced as she slowly rose to a sitting position, wings spread to rest on the ground on either side of her. "I suppose I have you to thank for that," she said in a warmer voice.

Nola's cheeks colored. "It was nothing," she said.

Kelty studied the girl. "We need to test this magic of yours. You drank more of the faerie essence." She did not say it like a question.

Nola nodded. "I have so much to tell you," she said in a voice full of dread. "Some of it you will not like."

"We both have secrets. Sharing them now will help us in the coming fight." Kelty's expression was determined and warm as she regarded Nola, but there was also a good amount of apprehension.

Nola nodded, tears shining in her eyes as she sat on the ground again. She fidgeted with a hole in her jeans.

"Speak," Kelty said.

Chapter 36

Seven days later

Nola concentrated on the soil beneath her toes, sending her power beneath her into the ground to mingle with the strands of energy already present. She reveled in the sensation as it responded to her, welcoming her. Now grounded, Nola beckoned to the power, bringing it back up into herself. She knelt to place her hand over a small mound of earth. Closing her eyes, she guided the power to the seed beneath. *Grow.* After a minute, she felt a tickle against her palm.

Joy spread through her at the green sprout that poked its way up beyond the soil.

"It grew! Just a little, but it grew!" Nola looked up into the tree beside her.

"Congratulations. You can now do magic like a faerie infant," Kelty called down dryly.

Nola shook her head, refusing to be cowed by the grumpy faerie. *She misses him.*

After she and Kelty spilled their secrets to each other, there was a bit of unease between the two. Nola couldn't tell what disturbed the faerie more: her agreement with Briar about the future proposition that she had agreed to in exchange for putting out the fire in the cabin, or that she kept it from Kelty. In turn, Kelty told Nola about her almost-relationship with Rowan and the likelihood that as the Star, she would now be the target of this group of faeries that the cloaks called their benefactors.

Despite the discomfort between them, Kelty demanded Nola return to the wood as soon as she was able so that they could assess her new power. Nola agreed, hoping this meant they would be able to get over the secrets and lies that were now out in the open to face the coming storm together.

Nola returned home directly afterward to parents that were furious at her for having stayed out all night and part of the day, for skipping school. She gave them vague answers, saying she fell asleep doing homework in the woods and didn't wake up until the middle of the next day. They bought her story, though they grounded her for two days. No phone and she was to come straight home after school. Those days were torture, but Nola reminded herself that she got off really easy. *They even felt bad grounding me. All the years of good behavior payed off.*

School the next day was interesting to say the least. Adam and Jeanine waited for Nola at the front of the school. They gave her apprehensive looks. *Why are they looking at me like that?* Nola wondered as she walked up the steps. *You would think they would be avoiding me.* And then Cameron joined them, giving her a hesitant smile as she approached.

"You look...good," he said a little nervously. There was another question in his eyes as well.

Nola nodded. "Everything's fine," she said a little awkwardly. Then, not knowing what to do, she walked past them into the school. *They're acting weird.*

The day got more complicated from there as others started to notice the weirdness of the group. Then they started whispering about where Derek was. *Great.* Nola cursed herself mentally for not thinking of this part. *We are all going to be suspected of murdering him. How am I the only one that understands that?*

At lunch, she marched up to the table where all three were sitting. They stared at her as she joined them.

"Look," she said in a low voice while trying to look casual. "Pretend everything is fine. We were supposed to meet Derek last night and he never showed. That's it."

Cameron looked down as he processed this. Adam and Jeanine gave her dumb looks. *This group was not picked for their brains.* "Derek is gone," she said in almost a whisper. "They will suspect us first."

Their eyes widened at that. "He really isn't coming back then," Adam said softly, looking a little lost.

Nola almost felt bad for him. Almost. "He got what he deserved," she said out loud.

Adam's eyes flashed across the table, but Cameron said, "He did, Adam. He tried to take them down. He started it. We never should have gotten involved in this. They are too powerful." He looked at Nola then. "And we should be glad Nola hasn't tried to destroy us yet."

Nola choked on her milk. She looked at them in surprise, all three staring back with a mix of trepidation and awe. *Right. I am the one with the power now.* She sat up straighter.

"Do as I say and maybe we will make it out of this alive," Nola told them.

Derek's absence became known the next day. Rumors ran amok in the school as authorities questioned them all. The police came out to the house and questioned Nola's father, who was luckily oblivious to the whole thing. To Nola's relief, the remaining cloaks stuck to the story that they were supposed to meet up with Derek and he never showed. *But will the authorities believe it,* Nola worried.

Once her punishment was lifted, Nola nervously walked across her yard and into the woods. *I hope Kelty has fully forgiven me. And I hope Rowan has returned. Or at least sent word. If he even can.* Her thoughts started to run together as she rounded the bend and Kelty's home tree came into sight.

Something about the place made her feel more at home than her actual home did. *Maybe I am more faerie than human now.*

The thought sent a thrill through her.

Nola knew the faerie was there, having caught a glimpse of Kelty in the trees above as she walked. *She looks well at least,* she thought as the faerie touched down lightly in front of her.

They stared at each other hesitantly. Then Kelty nodded. "Welcome back," she said with no trace of wariness or animosity.

Nola felt an answering warmth spread through her. "Thank you."

Then the work began. Neither knew what was coming, but that did not mean they could not prepare themselves. Kelty worked to neutralize or repurpose the magic of the vials taken from the humans. She tested Nola, poking and prodding her with her own magic, then making her attempt to influence the *ara* around them. Nola failed miserably at first, distracted by worries from her human life and of Briar.

There had been no sign of him since she threatened him with the knife she now kept on her. *But he will be back, and I will be more prepared this time.*

Kelty slapped her lightly on the cheek to break her out of her thoughts. "You are not thinking clearly. Get to a place where all that matters is you and the *ara*. Only then can you properly connect to it."

Cheek stinging, Nola nodded, both chagrined and a little amused by the stern shorter being.

Nola improved day by day, but Kelty still grew more agitated. She tended to start pacing while Nola tried to get in the right head space and looked about to yell or curse when the girl failed. She did neither, but Nola could see the plants around the faerie quiver in response to her agitation.

"He will come back," Nola told Kelty one day when she caught her frowning off into the distance.

"What?" Kelty snapped her head around.

"Rowan. He will come back."

"How do you know, human girl?" Kelty challenged.

"I saw the way he looked at you," Nola said, choosing to ignore the use of the *human girl* label. "As soon as he is able, he will come back," she told the faerie with confidence.

Kelty said nothing, turning her head to gaze off into the distance again. With a sigh, Nola went back to concentrating.

"What will you do when Briar returns?" The faerie's question broke into her mind again.

Well, isn't that a loaded question. I guess we are not over that one quite yet. Opening her eyes, she looked directly into Kelty's piercing ones.

"I don't know, but whatever it is, I won't let it come between us again. I think we need to stick together and be a team if we are to survive whatever is coming."

Nola meant the words. She still dreamed of Briar, feelings for him a confused muddle. *Sometimes I'm sure I never want to see him again. Other times I can't wait until he shows up. I'm a mess about it, which is never a good thing.*

Kelty stared for a moment more, before a look of approval crossed her face.

Relieved, Nola blurted out the question before thinking. "Do you still want to go back to Faerie? I mean, if you could, would you go? Here isn't so bad, is it?" *Way to sound like a whiny child.* Nola looked away in embarrassment.

There was a pause.

"I have unfinished business here," was the reply she got. Nola turned her eyes back to Kelty to see a sort of calm come over her face.

It's a faerie non-answer, but I'll take it. Nola smiled and hesitantly extended a hand. "Sisters, then?"

The faerie quirked up an eyebrow. "You are not my sister."

"I mean chosen sisters," Nola said with a laugh. "We make a pact here to never let guys come between us. Or evil faeries or humans or whatever. Like sisters. We fight together."

Nola waited with her hand extended as a myriad of emotions cycled through the faerie's face. Surprise and skepticism gave way to something like fear and indecision, and then something like warmth and gratitude took over.

The faerie reached out her hand to grasp Nola's.

"Sisters," Kelty agreed.

Chapter 37

Kelty's gaze swept the wood as she flew. The place seemed brighter. Even the humans looked more peaceful without the dark magic seeping into the life of her place of banishment.

Peace in the wood.

It was Kelty's goal. The way she would earn her place back in Faerie.

Now, it was so much more complicated.

The *ara* coiled within her answered her call as strong as before, despite her interactions with Nola and being around the other humans. Though that didn't guarantee she could be welcomed back to Faerie, especially since being touched by the dark magic and the iron poison. For all Kelty knew, other faeries would sense a human taint to her that she did not.

Kelty landed lightly on the branch that had the view of the green field many of the visitors of the park used to play games. As her gaze scanned those gathered below in small clusters, she remembered the family of four that had brought up such painful memories before she saw Nola for the first time.

She sighed as she sat, resting her head back against tree trunk. *I was so bent on hating this world. And now I have given my name to a human.*

Their kind still irked her, but there was at least one human deserving of her protection.

She also had personal business to settle in this world.

Kelty bested the dark magic, but that meant nothing while the faction of outcasts was still lurking. They took Rowan and almost killed him. They would pay for that.

Revenge was easier to focus on than worrying and contemplating the possibility that Rowan was dead, that the iron poison of the cage had gotten to him like Derek's knife had to her, that the faeries were not able to heal him like Nola had healed her. Kelty shuddered and closed off her mind to those thoughts.

He is alive, she told herself. *And he will come when he is able.*

A flare in the *ara* of the wood that meant the presence of a faerie broke her out of her thoughts.

Kelty's heart leapt into her throat as she spread her wings and took off. *Please, let it be him.*

As she neared, however, it became clear that the presence was not her potential. Retreating within herself and putting on a hard exterior, Kelty landed lightly in front of an unfamiliar faerie.

He had the mark of the Day on his temple with skin of dusty gold and wings of white. His long white hair was tied behind his head in a messy bun, a few strands escaping to frame a long face with high cheekbones and large eyes. The garment he wore wrapped around his tall, willowy body from neck to ankle, much like Briar did, was a light beige. He stared down at her, one hand on his hip, expression in his golden eyes was somewhat mocking, as if he knew what was in store for her.

The faerie who looked so out of place in her wood, like a lost beam of sunlight, extended one hand delicately. "Kelty of the Night, you are summoned to the Court of Outcasts," he said in a soft, almost feminine voice.

Kelty's back straightened and she flicked her wings at the word *summoned.* As if she had done something wrong and needed to go to her punishment.

Court of Outcasts. But this is what she'd been waiting for. Kelty smirked at the gold faerie as she laid her palm upon his. Heat burned as light enveloped their hands for a brief flash. Without looking, she knew her palm now bore a mark on it. A summons. A magical binding that would cause her intense pain if she ignored its call.

The gold faerie nodded, cocky smile still in place, then took off into the air.

Kelty let him go without even checking his flight path. This faerie was a spirit user, a messenger meant to mark her and do nothing more. The mark would lead her to them when they wanted her, to the enemy.

She turned her hand over to regard the symbol of black on her palm: the sun and moon combined, but with a jagged slash through it. *They dare to mar the symbol of Faerie.*

"So it begins."

Kelty froze, eyes widening at the smooth male voice that drifted out of the trees behind her. She inhaled the scent of soil and the forest and growing things.

Rowan. A warmth spread through her, yet she couldn't stop the fearful thoughts that intruded on her joy. *What if we are no longer potentials? What if things have changed?*

She closed her eyes, trying to gather the courage to turn around and face him.

A light wind buffeted her wings as he landed behind her. "Star," he said softly.

Kelty's eyes snapped open and she whirled around to look up

188

into Rowan's face. Her fears almost vanished at the sight of him, that calm expression and warm smile.

The warmth within her core intensified at the brightness swirling at his core. Not quite partners yet, but still potentials.

"Rowan," she breathed his name.

Then Kelty caught sight of the black scar that ran in a jagged line across the center of his bare chest.

"What happened? They could not heal it?" Kelty demanded as she scanned the rest of him, stepping around his back to see Rowan's wings, needing to erase the memory of them torn and covered in silver. *Whole again,* she thought with relief as she finished her inspection.

"The faerie were able to draw out the poison through this wound." He indicated the mark on his chest. "But they could not change the discoloration. I was lucky it healed at all."

Kelty reached up a tentative hand to trace the mark. The skin was slightly raised and warm to the touch. "Did they at least get it all out? Your magic has not been affected?"

"Yes," he answered, his warm eyes looking into hers. "It took days, but they drove it out."

Kelty's eyes rose to the Telk stone hanging around his neck. She dropped her hand. "So you are not an outcast, though you are tainted." Jealousy rose in her throat despite her efforts to push it down.

"Yes," he sighed, running a hand over his face. "Not many will go near me. But I am not an outcast either. The one who survived," he trailed off, a distant look crossing his face.

"They fear you." Kelty let out a sigh. "And the human world would not be much of a punishment for one who knows how to defeat the humans. It is probably the best you could hope for."

But what does it mean for us? The question echoed in her mind.

189

Kelty stepped back. She looked straight into his brown eyes. "Why did you come back?"

Surprise flicked across his face at the question. Kelty crossed her arms, though, needing to hear the words.

"I do not know what my future holds, but I know I want you in it," Rowan said finally. Then his expression hardened. "And those outcasts will pay for trying to sacrifice me. I will not be caught off guard this time."

Tears pricked at Kelty's eyes. She stepped forward and threw her arms around him. He returned the embrace, murmuring in her ear, "So you are happy to see me."

"I want you to be a part of my future," she whispered the words through happy tears. "Those outcasts will pay. Did you see any of them?"

"No. I saw nothing."

Kelty frowned. They would have to watch their backs around these outcasts.

"I told you he would come back," a voice drifted from the path, cutting into the moment.

Hastily, Kelty broke the embrace and stepped back. "You have terrible timing, Nola," she said in annoyance.

Nola smiled as she stepped over a bush and into the clearing. "Sorry," she said in a voice that did not sound that way.

Rowan peered at the girl. "You are a little more faerie, human girl."

"And you are a little more human," Nola shot back at him good-naturedly as she peered at the scar. "Looks nice."

The green faerie gave her a look. "Nice?"

"Yeah, scars make you look rugged."

A sense of peace and belonging settled into Kelty as she listened to their playful exchange. They were the family she never asked for, the family that chose her despite her shortcomings.

Nola looked over at her, brow furrowing. "What's that on your palm, Kelty?" She grabbed the faerie's hand and turned it over.

Kelty looked past Nola to lock eyes with Rowan. His answering gaze filled her with hope and strength.

"The beginning," Kelty answered.

From the Author

Thank you for reading The Nameless!

If you have a few moments, I would really appreciate it if you could leave me an honest review on Amazon. Even just a sentence or two really helps out authors like me. You can either search for The Nameless by Allison Rose or visit www.amazon.com/dp/B07LC4D1HY.

Again, thank you. The opinions of readers really mean the world to me.

Happy reading,
  Allison Rose

Acknowledgments

Thank you to everyone who believed in me throughout the creation of this book. I would be nowhere without my family, friends, editors, and other writers whose encouragement has got me through days where I wanted to quit.

A special thank you to my fiancé, Gary, for putting up with me while I spent a lot of my free time working towards this dream. And also my mom, my biggest cheerleader.

To Loni, Ashley, Alex, Amanda, Naomi, Pagan, and the members of the launch team, I couldn't have done this without you. Your advise and expertise has always been exactly what I needed.

Last but not least, thank you to all the readers out there who believe that books are magic. You give me hope.

About the Author

Driven by a lifelong passion for words and reading fantasy novels, Allison Rose writes YA fantasy stories featuring faeries, magic, and female heroines. She has a BA in psychology and is fascinated by how other people think, but her love for reading and writing is greater. When Allison isn't writing, she is proofreading the works of others. Allison lives with her fiancé, collie mix, bunny, and chinchilla in the place of wild weather also known as Buffalo, New York.

You can connect with me on:
- http://www.allisonroseauthor.com
- http://www.facebook.com/allisonroseauthor
- http://www.instagram.com/allison.rose.author

Subscribe to my newsletter:
- http://eepurl.com/de-nQL

Also by Allison Rose

Want to know how it all started? Read Discovery for free by signing up for my newsletter at www.allisonroseauthor.com.

Discovery

Sixteen-year-old Nola's life would never be the same again.

When Nola steals a magical life-giving substance from her father's basement lab, his intern, Derek, blackmails her into bringing the substance to the woods after dark.

She leaves that night as an unwilling member of a cult-like group, forever changed and now aware of the threat of dark magic concocted by careless teens and an otherworldly being much like the faeries of fictional stories.

Nola's eyes were now open. If only she could see a way out.

Made in the USA
San Bernardino, CA
29 January 2019